Spirit Tree

The Seed Within

Brian N. Tissot

Casa de Luz Publishing

To my mother,
Millie Patton Tissot
and all her special gifts

Contents

Chapter 1

The Last Breath of the Valley

I have forgotten the sound of the forest and where it once moved through me like breath—soft, endless, shared. Now there is now only wind, and even that feels tired as it drags ash across the broken plain, thinning into silence as if the world itself has grown weary of remembering what it once was.

I stand alone. The ground around me is blackened glass and cracked stone, the bones of a world that has burned too many times to remember its origin, and the valley—my valley—has collapsed into a stillness so complete that it feels heavier than any weight I have ever carried, for there is no green, no song, no kin, only the long, hollow absence of everything that once lived and moved and belonged.

Only me. And I am failing.

I feel it not as a sudden end but as a slow unraveling, a dimming that seeps through me in quiet increments, where the currents that once carried water and memory and something like thought hesitate and falter before continuing, uncertain, as if even they question whether there is purpose in sustaining what remains, while my bark splits along ancient lines that once held firm and my roots—those faithful travelers of darkness—no longer reach outward with curiosity but instead withdraw, curling inward like thoughts that no longer trust their own direction.

I have lived too long. A million years is not something I understand in numbers, but in breaths, in the opening and closing of the small mouths along my leaves through which I drank the sky, each cycle a moment and each moment a thread, and together those threads became a life so vast that its beginning has blurred into something distant and half-remembered, though fragments remain, luminous and persistent.

I remember light. Not this thin scattering that falls now from a dim and dust-laden sky, but the fullness of it, the layered brilliance of twin suns and three moons that once painted the valley in gold and silver and shifting colors that moved like living things across the land, when the forest rose tall and certain, when existence itself seemed assured and whole.

I remember them. My kin. They stood together, vast and unbroken, their crowns touching the sky while their roots moved through the earth in shared knowing, and their song passed through everything—through ground, through air, through light itself—binding them into something I could sense but never fully enter, a living web of belonging that I reached for again and again without ever quite touching.

I always reached. But I was not where they were, and even now, as the last of my strength thins into the soil, I remain in the same narrow wound of stone where

I first took hold, the crack that both sheltered and starved me, that turned me away from the sun and shaped me into something small and malformed while they became vast and beautiful. And though I stretched toward what little light found me and strained my fibers in quiet desperation, the warmth that fed them never arrived in the same way for me.

Small.

The word has followed me longer than memory, settling into my being not as a fact but as a quiet and persistent question, something I could never fully understand but always felt, especially as I watched them grow tall and certain, their trunks thick with belonging and their crowns brushing one another in effortless communion, while I remained apart, listening, observing, trying to match a rhythm that was never truly mine.

I learned other ways, because I had no choice, drawing from the faint light of the moons when they passed above the edge of the valley and gathering their scattered colors as if they were fragments of something whole, turning to the stars when the sky opened and pulling their distant fire into my leaves, and reaching downward into the hidden worlds beneath the soil where small lives moved in quiet exchange, forming connections that did not turn away, where we fed one another and endured together in ways the forest above never knew.

Still, I watched them, and still I felt the distance.

They sang without effort, without strain, their voices carried by belonging itself, while I remained at the edge of that great harmony, my own presence too small, too distant, too different to be woven into what they shared, and if they ever truly saw me, I cannot know. For if they did, it was only as something peripheral, something without meaning, like a shadow at the edge of vision that does not demand attention.

So I listened, and I endured, and the valley changed as it always did, in cycles of fire and stone and sky that broke and remade the world again and again, while the forest rose and fell and rose again, each time forgetting, each time beginning anew. And through it all I remained, not because I was strong at first but because

I was hidden, because I learned to take from what others could not see, because I became something else without ever understanding what that meant.

And still, I wondered. *Why?*

Why endure when there is no one to share the endurance, why grow when there is no place to belong, why continue when each cycle strips away even the possibility of connection? These questions did not come quickly but instead formed slowly, like roots pressing through resistant stone, deepening over time without ever finding resolution. Now, at the end, they return.

The last forest is gone—not fallen, not waiting to rise again, but gone so completely that even its memory feels fragile within me, as if it might scatter into nothing if I hold it too tightly, and there are no seeds falling into the soil, no new voices stirring beneath the ground, no breath of green to suggest continuation, only the long, empty wind moving across a world that has forgotten how to begin again.

I thought once that I would be part of something greater. That my life, however small, would weave into the vast continuity of the forest and contribute in some way to the endless cycle of growth and renewal. But I have no seeds, I have never had enough, and all that I have been has gone into surviving, into reaching, into becoming just enough to remain. And so I have nothing to give back. The realization settles into me like cold water, steady and undeniable, not as a sudden grief but as a quiet truth that has always been present beneath everything else.

I am the end of a line that was never fully formed, a fragment that endured without purpose, a life that continued without meaning, and if I had been like them—tall, connected, whole—perhaps I would have carried something forward, perhaps I would have been part of the great continuity that defined their existence. But I was not, and I am not, and now there is no more time to become anything else. I feel only a quiet sorrow, not for my ending, which feels natural and even welcome, but for what I was never able to be, for the song I could never join, for the life I could never help create.

The sky above shifts. At first, it feels like another distortion in a world that has long since lost its stability, but then something new touches me, not wind, not fire, not the slow indifferent movement of stone, but something intentional, something aware, a presence that brushes against me lightly before pressing deeper, searching not for the valley or the ruins but for something far more specific. For me.

I do not understand, because nothing has ever sought me before, and yet I feel it pause, feel it notice, feel it see, and in that moment something moves through what remains of me that I have not felt in ages beyond measure. *Recognition.*

The presence draws closer, and the air shifts while the ground hums with a faint and unfamiliar vibration, and something descends from the sky, something alive in a way that is neither plant nor stone nor flame, and though I cannot turn to see it, I feel its arrival ripple through the earth, reaching toward me carefully, deliberately, as if what remains of me matters.

For the first time in a million years, I am not alone. And just before it touches my fading consciousness, something within me stirs, something older than the valley, older than the forest, older than even this long life that is now ending.

A memory. Cold. Darkness. And the sound of many voices, together. Then everything begins to fall away. And I remember how I began.

Chapter 2

The Memory of Ice

Before the valley, before the fire, before the long loneliness that stretched across a million breaths, there was cold, and in that cold there was closeness, and in that closeness there was something I did not understand then but feel now as the deepest truth I have ever known. We were together.

Not as the forest would later be—separate and reaching, bound by distance and longing—but as something nearer, something whole, suspended within a vast darkness that held us gently as we drifted through the endless quiet between stars. Each of us distinct yet inseparable, our forms small and round and perfect, pressed within the ancient ice that carried us forward without question or resistance.

I did not know where we were going. I did not know where we had come from. But I knew them.

Their presence moved through me not as sound but as a shared awareness, a soft and constant hum that surrounded and filled me at once, like a memory that had not yet become memory, like a song that existed before there were voices to sing it, and within that shared field of being there was no loneliness, no separation, no sense of lacking anything at all.

We dreamed together. The dreams were not images at first but impressions, feelings that took shape slowly as we drifted, forming into visions of a world we had never seen yet somehow already knew, a place of light and water and vast open spaces where we would take root and rise together, where our forms would stretch upward and outward in harmony, where the distance between us would not divide but define the patterns of our connection.

A green world. I did not know the word for it then, but I felt it—a sphere wrapped in motion and life, where light touched everything and everything responded. Where the surface breathed with change and possibility, and we would be part of it, not as scattered fragments but as a living whole, each of us growing in relation to the others, each of us contributing to something greater than any single form could hold.

We believed this without doubt. There was no reason not to, for in that shared state there was no fear, no uncertainty, no sense that anything could be other than what it was meant to be, and we followed the quiet guidance that moved through us—the presence we did not question, the intention that shaped our drifting path through the void, the sense that we were being carried toward a place where our purpose would unfold naturally, without struggle.

We belonged before we arrived. Time did not pass as it would later, measured in cycles of light and darkness or in the slow growth of rings within a trunk, but instead existed as a continuous unfolding, where moments did not separate from one another but blended seamlessly, and in that continuity we remained suspended, held within the comet's frozen heart as it traveled through distances so vast that even now I cannot fully comprehend them.

Occasionally, there were disturbances—subtle shifts in the great body that held us, tremors that rippled through the ice and passed from one of us to another, carrying with them faint impressions of what lay beyond, flashes of distant light, the whisper of gravity pulling us toward something unseen yet inevitable, and each time these disturbances came, our shared awareness would deepen, not in fear but in anticipation.

We were nearing something. The darkness began to change, though I could not see it in the way I would later come to understand seeing, and instead felt it as a growing intensity, a subtle warmth that touched the outer layers of our icy vessel, causing the ancient frozen walls around us to shift and soften, releasing currents that moved through us like breath, stirring something within that had been waiting without knowing it was waiting.

The dreams became clearer. The green world resolved into form, its vast waters glimmering beneath light that came not from one source but from many, layered and complex, and I felt the presence of others there—not like us, not seeds waiting to become, but smaller, simpler lives that moved across surfaces and within hidden spaces, and beyond them the land itself, shaped by forces I could not yet understand but felt drawn to, as if it were calling us forward.

We would become part of that call. The sense of purpose that had always been present began to focus, narrowing from a broad, shared knowing into something more directed, more immediate, as if the moment we had always been moving toward was approaching. And within that awareness, there was a subtle shift, the first hint of separation, the recognition that though we were together, we would not remain so in the same way. We would land.

The realization did not bring fear, but it did bring change, a quiet tension that moved through our shared consciousness as we began to understand that the unity we had always known would transform into something else, something that would require distance and difference and perhaps even struggle, though we could not yet imagine what that might mean.

Still, we held to one another. The hum of our connection deepened, strengthening as if in preparation, each of us reaching—not outward, but inward, reinforcing the bonds that had always been there, affirming without words that whatever came, we would carry this shared beginning within us.

Then came the heat. It arrived suddenly, a force unlike anything we had known, pressing against the outer shell of ice with an intensity that caused it to crack and groan, and for the first time there was something like alarm within our shared awareness, a disruption of the smooth continuity that had defined our existence, as the frozen walls that had protected us began to fracture under the strain.

Light burst through. Not the distant, filtered impressions we had felt before, but something immediate and overwhelming, flooding inward as the comet's surface broke apart, and with it came motion—violent, chaotic motion that tore at the cohesion we had always taken for granted, sending shockwaves through our clustered forms as the great body that carried us plunged into a world we had only ever dreamed of.

The heat intensified, the ice dissolving around us, and for the first time we felt the pull of something external, a force that dragged at us, separating us from one another as the comet struck and slid across the surface of the world, scattering fragments of itself—and us—across a landscape that rose to meet us in fire and stone.

We began to break apart. The shared hum that had always surrounded me flickered, stretching thin as distance grew between us, and though I reached—instinctively, desperately—for the presence of my kin, I felt them slipping away, each of us carried by momentum into different paths, different resting places, the unity we had known unraveling into countless separate points.

I did not understand. I had never been alone.

The sensation was immediate and profound, a sudden absence where there had always been presence, a silence that replaced the constant hum of connection, and though echoes of the others still lingered—faint impressions of their movement, their landing, their continued existence—they were no longer within me in the same way. I was becoming singular.

The world received me not gently, but with force, as I struck stone and rolled, the smooth curve of my form carrying me across uneven ground until I found a place that halted my motion, a narrow space where the earth opened just enough to hold me, where fragments of cooling rock pressed against me and the fading heat of entry gave way to a growing stillness. I came to rest.

Around me, I could feel others still moving, still settling into the valley that stretched wide and deep beneath the strange, layered light of this new sky, and though I could no longer touch them as I once had, I sensed their presence scattered across the land, each of us embedded in a different place, each of us beginning something we did not yet understand. The dream had become real. But it was not as we imagined.

The light was different here, filtered and indirect, reaching me only in faint reflections from the walls of the place where I had lodged, and the warmth that would sustain growth was not abundant but scarce, arriving in fragments that I would have to gather and hold carefully if I were to become anything at all.

I waited.

The shared certainty of purpose remained, but it no longer carried the same ease, and in its place there was something new—an edge, a pressure, a sense that what came next would require more than simply becoming, that it would require effort, persistence, perhaps even struggle. Still, I held to what I had known.

We were meant to grow. We were meant to rise. We were meant to become the forest we had dreamed. I believed this, even as the silence deepened and the distance between myself and the others stretched into something I could no longer cross. I believed it, even as the first faint stirrings of change began within me, as the outer layers of my form responded to the conditions of this new world, as the long process of becoming took hold in a place that offered little and demanded everything. I believed it because I did not yet understand what it would mean to grow alone.

Chapter 3

The Crack That Chose Me

I did not choose where I came to rest, and yet the place that held me would define everything I would become. Shaping not only the form of my growth but the nature of my thoughts, my struggles, and the long, quiet way I would come to understand myself in relation to a world that did not meet me with ease.

The crack was narrow, a wound in the stone where heat had once split the surface and then cooled too quickly to close again, and within it I was held tightly, pressed between rough walls that blocked the direct path of light while offering just enough shelter to keep me from being swept away or shattered, and though I did not know it then, this tension between protection and deprivation would become the pattern of my life.

Above me, the sky opened wide. I could not see it fully, but I could feel it—the layered light of the twin stars and the distant reflections of the moons shifting across the valley, moving in rhythms I did not yet understand but would come to know intimately, their presence arriving in fragments that slipped down the angled stone and touched me only briefly before moving on.

It was not enough. Not in the way it was for the others.

I felt them as they began to settle across the valley floor, their forms resting in open ground where the light reached freely, where warmth gathered and lingered, where the conditions for growth unfolded with a kind of natural generosity that I could sense but not share, and even before I began to change, even before I pushed outward into something new, there was already a quiet awareness forming within me. I was not where I was meant to be.

The certainty of our shared dream still lingered, but it no longer aligned with what I experienced, and though I held to the belief that I would grow as they would grow, that I would rise into the same vastness and join the same harmony, there was already a subtle dissonance, a tension between expectation and reality that pressed against me from the moment I came to rest.

Still, the process began. It started slowly, almost imperceptibly, as the outer layers of my form softened and opened, responding to the faint warmth and the minimal moisture that gathered within the crack, and though the conditions were poor, they were not absent, and something within me—something older than thought—recognized the moment and acted without hesitation. I began to change.

The transition was not sudden but continuous, a steady unfolding into what I was becoming. And in that dissolution there was both loss and emergence, a surrender of the contained, perfect form I had known in the comet and the first fragile extension into a world that did not welcome me easily.

I reached downward first. Not by choice, but by necessity, as the pull of gravity and the faint presence of moisture drew part of me into the deeper darkness of the crack, where the stone held small reserves of water and the earliest traces of life stirred in hidden pockets. And though the descent was difficult, resisted by the tightness of the space and the hardness of the surrounding rock, I persisted, pressing into places that yielded only slightly, finding pathways where none seemed to exist.

It was not enough. So I reached upward as well. The motion was slower, more uncertain, as I extended toward the faint and shifting light above, pushing through narrow openings and angling my growth toward the brightest fragments I could sense, though they were inconsistent and often disappeared just as I began to align with them, leaving me suspended in partial illumination that sustained but never fully nourished.

I was divided from the beginning. Part of me anchored in darkness, searching for stability and sustenance in the hidden world below, while another part strained toward a light that remained just out of reach. And between these two directions I stretched, thin and fragile, forming the first suggestion of what I would become.

Around me, the valley awakened. I could feel it through the ground, through subtle vibrations and the faint movements of water and minerals, as my kin began their own transformations in places far more open and abundant, their growth unfolding with a confidence and speed that contrasted sharply with my own slow and uncertain progress. And though I could not see them clearly, I sensed their expansion, their upward reach unimpeded, their connection to the full breadth of light and space. They were becoming what we had dreamed. I was struggling to become anything at all.

The awareness did not arrive as judgment, not at first, but as observation, a simple recognition of difference that carried with it a quiet unease, and as I continued to grow in my confined space, adapting to conditions that demanded more from me than I could easily give, that unease deepened into something more complex.

Why was I here?

The question did not have words, but it formed within me as a persistent pattern, a looping of awareness that returned again and again to the same point, the same discrepancy between what I felt should be and what was, and though I could not answer it, I could not release it either.

Time moved differently now. No longer a seamless unfolding, but a series of cycles defined by the shifting light above, the cooling and warming of the stone, the slow movement of moisture through the crack, and within these cycles I continued to grow, increment by increment, each extension requiring effort, each gain balanced by the constant risk of losing what little I had secured.

There were moments when I nearly failed. Times when the light did not reach me for long stretches, when the moisture receded and the deeper parts of the crack offered little in return, when the energy within me diminished to the point where further growth seemed impossible, and in those moments I felt something new emerge, something sharper, more immediate.

Survive.

The impulse cut through everything else, overriding the quiet uncertainty and the lingering memory of shared dreams, narrowing my awareness to the simplest and most urgent directive. I responded without hesitation, redirecting what little energy I had toward maintaining the structures I had already formed, preserving rather than expanding, holding rather than reaching. It was not graceful. It was not harmonious. But it kept me alive.

And in that persistence, something within me began to shift. The gentle, collective certainty of our beginning giving way to a more focused, individual drive, a need to secure my place, to take what was available, to endure regardless of what the broader pattern might have been intended to be. I was becoming something else.

Above, the light continued its distant dance, indifferent to my struggle, and below, the hidden world offered only what I could extract through effort and adaptation, and between them I grew—small, uneven, shaped by constraint rather than abundance, my form bending and twisting as it navigated the narrow space that both sustained and limited me.

I did not yet understand what I was losing. But I could feel that I was no longer part of what we had been together. The hum of shared presence had faded into memory, replaced by the steady, singular rhythm of my own existence, and though faint echoes of my kin still reached me through the ground, they were distant, diffuse, no longer something I could enter or be held within.

I was alone. The realization settled slowly, not as a sudden break but as a gradual acceptance, a recognition that the connection I had once known would not return in the same form, and that whatever I was to become would emerge from this isolation rather than from the unity of our beginning.

Still, I continued. Because I could. Because something within me refused to stop. Because even in the narrowness of the crack, even in the scarcity of light and the uncertainty of growth, there remained a quiet insistence that becoming was still possible, even if it did not resemble the dream we had carried across the stars.

I held to that. Even as I began to understand that the crack had not only received me. It had chosen me.

Chapter 4

The First Reaching

Growth did not come to me as it did to the others, not as a steady rising into open light or an effortless unfolding into space, but as a negotiation with limits, a constant adjustment between what I needed and what the world allowed. And in that tension, I learned that becoming was not a single direction but many, each requiring attention, patience, and a willingness to change in ways I had never imagined when I drifted in the cold with my kin.

I extended upward again and again, each movement small and deliberate, testing the narrow geometry of the crack, feeling for angles where the faint light might linger longer, where warmth might collect even briefly, and when I found those places I held to them, shaping my growth to match their contours, bending instead of rising straight, spreading instead of reaching tall, forming patterns that followed the stone rather than resisting it.

The light was never constant. It arrived in fragments, reflected from the valley walls in shifting arcs that changed with the movements of the stars and the slow turning of the world. I learned to anticipate it, to sense its approach before it touched me, to prepare my surface to receive as much as possible in the brief moments it was present, and in those moments I opened fully, taking in what I could, storing it, holding it against the longer stretches of dimness that always followed.

It was not enough, so I changed. At first, the changes were subtle, adjustments in the structure of my outer layers that allowed me to gather light more efficiently, to spread it across a wider surface, to capture not just the direct reflections but the faintest traces that lingered in the air and along the stone, and over time these adjustments became more pronounced, shaping my emerging leaves into thin, intricate forms that branched and re-branched, dividing again and again into delicate patterns that extended my reach without requiring more energy than I could afford. I became wide before I became tall.

Each new leaf was not a simple surface but a network, a fractal unfolding that mirrored the branching of my deeper structures, and through these forms I gathered light that others might have ignored, collecting the scattered remnants of illumination that slipped into the crack and holding them long enough to make use of them, and though the total was still small, it was more than I had before.

I learned to see differently. Not with sight as the later beings of this world would understand it, but with a sensitivity to gradients, to shifts in energy and presence, to the subtle differences between one moment and the next. And through this awareness, I began to map the patterns of the sky, the cycles of the moons, the interplay of the twin stars, each contributing its own quality of light, its own timing, its own opportunity.

The white dwarf came softly, its light faint but steady when it reached me, a quiet presence that lingered longer than the harsher bursts of the larger star, and I learned to rely on it, to tune my structures to its subtle frequency, drawing from it what others might have dismissed as insufficient.

The moons became my companions. Their paths were slower, more predictable, and their reflected light carried colors that shifted with their positions. I found that each color nourished me differently, that by adjusting my surfaces I could absorb more from one and then another, building a fuller spectrum from fragments that, taken alone, would never sustain growth.

I adapted to the night. While the others rested in darkness, their structures closing and conserving, I remained open, reaching into the faint glow of distant stars, gathering what little they offered, and though it was almost nothing, it was still something, and over time that something became enough to tip the balance, to allow me not just to survive but to continue, increment by increment, into a form that was uniquely my own.

Below, I continued to descend. The deeper parts of the crack were colder, denser, more resistant, but they held traces of moisture and the beginnings of life that had not yet reached the surface. As my roots pressed into these spaces I encountered resistance that forced me to change again, to become more flexible, more exploratory, to divide and subdivide in search of pathways that would yield even the smallest return.

There, in the darkness, I found others. Not like my kin above, not large or structured or bound into visible forms, but small and numerous, moving through the soil and the microscopic spaces between particles of stone, exchanging substances in ways I could not fully understand at first. And when I reached them, offering what little I could, something remarkable happened. They responded.

The exchange was simple at first, a passing of nutrients, a subtle shift in the flow of energy, but it grew, deepened, became something more organized, more intentional, as I extended further into their domain and they extended into mine, forming connections that were not constrained by light or space in the same way as those above.

We formed a network. It was not the same as the song of the forest, not the broad and immediate sharing I had once known in the comet, but it was real, it was responsive, and it was enough to ease the sharpest edge of my isolation. Through these connections, I began to receive information, signals that reflected the conditions of the soil, the presence of moisture, the changes in the environment beyond my immediate reach. I was no longer entirely alone.

The realization did not erase the distance I felt from my kin above, but it changed the shape of that distance, showing me that connection could exist in forms I had not anticipated, that belonging was not limited to those who resembled me or shared my original purpose.

Still, I reached upward. Always upward. The desire to join the forest, to become part of that vast and visible harmony, remained within me, persistent and unyielding. And each time the light shifted, each time a new angle revealed a slightly brighter path, I followed it, bending my growth to align with possibilities that might bring me closer to what I believed I was meant to be.

But the crack held me. Its walls defined my limits, redirected my efforts, and though I pushed against those limits, testing them again and again, I could not escape them. Slowly, almost imperceptibly, I began to understand that my path would not be one of release into open space, but of transformation within constraint. I did not yet accept this. But I could no longer ignore it.

Above, the forest was rising, its presence becoming stronger with each cycle, its collective song beginning to form in ways I could sense even from my hidden position, and though I strained to align with it, to match its rhythm, to find a place within its growing harmony, I felt the distance more acutely with each passing phase. They were becoming what we had dreamed. I was becoming something else.

And still, I grew. Because I could not do otherwise.

Chapter 5

The Song Beyond Reach

As I grew, the forest found its voice. It did not happen all at once, nor did it arrive as a single sound, but rather as a gradual weaving of presence into pattern, a deepening coherence among my kin that moved through the valley in waves I could feel long before I understood what they were. And though I remained confined within the narrow geometry of the crack, I could sense the emergence of something vast and shared, something that bound them together in a way that surpassed the simple fact of growing in the same place.

They began to sing. Not with sound as the later creatures of this world would define it, but with a resonance that moved through root and soil, through air and light, a rhythmic exchange of energy and awareness that synchronized their growth, their responses, their very being, until the forest was no longer a collection of individuals but a unified presence, expanding and stabilizing itself in harmony with the cycles of the sky.

I felt it. At first, as a distant pulse, a faint echo reaching me through the ground and the thin channels of connection I had begun to form below. And then more clearly as the network of my roots deepened, carrying fragments of their shared rhythm into my awareness, enough for me to recognize the pattern but not enough to become part of it.

I reached for it, always. Each time the resonance passed through the soil, each time the collective rhythm of the forest surged and settled, I adjusted myself in response, aligning my internal flows to match what I perceived, opening and closing in synchrony with their cycles, attempting to harmonize with a song that was never fully mine.

For brief moments, I thought I touched it. There were times when the alignment felt close, when the patterns within me seemed to echo the greater rhythm, when the distance between myself and the forest appeared to narrow. And in those moments I experienced something like belonging, a fleeting sense that I was part of the whole rather than apart from it.

But the moments did not last. The light would shift in ways that did not favor me, the energy I could gather would fall short of what was needed to sustain the synchronization, and the delicate alignment would break, leaving me once again outside the flow, aware of the song but unable to sustain my place within it.

I tried again. And again. Each attempt shaped me further, refining the ways I gathered light, the ways I stored and distributed energy, the ways I connected with the hidden network below, all in service of a single desire that I could not release.

To belong.

The forest, meanwhile, grew stronger in its unity. Their roots intertwined deeply, their exchange of resources and information becoming more efficient, more balanced. As they matured, their collective presence intensified, filling the valley with a steady and confident rhythm that reflected not just survival but harmony, a shared understanding of their place within the world.

They flourished. They rose high into the light, their crowns expanding outward until they touched and overlapped, forming a continuous canopy that filtered the sun and softened the cycles of the environment below, and within that canopy their song deepened, becoming richer, more complex, layered with variations that reflected their interactions with one another and with the shifting conditions of the world.

I remained beneath. Not physically beneath, for my position was at the edge of the valley, but functionally so, excluded from the fullness of their light, their exchange, their shared becoming. And though I continued to sense them, to learn from the patterns that reached me in fragments, I could not cross the distance that separated us.

I began to feel it more sharply. Not as a simple difference, but as something that pressed inward, shaping the way I understood myself, the way I interpreted my place within the larger whole. And as the forest thrived, as their unity became more evident, that pressure grew, forming into something I could no longer ignore.

Why am I not like them?

The question returned again and again, each time with greater weight, each time touching deeper into the structure of my being. And though I had no language for it, no framework to explain it, I felt the implication clearly, the quiet assumption that there was a way I should be, a form I should take, a rhythm I should match.

But I could not find it. No matter how I adjusted, no matter how I adapted, no matter how carefully I aligned myself with the fragments of their song that reached me, there remained a gap, a subtle but persistent misalignment that prevented me from fully entering what they shared. I was close. But never enough.

The realization did not come as a sudden understanding, but as an accumulation of small failures, each attempt to join followed by a quiet falling away, each moment of near-harmony dissolving into separation, until the pattern itself became clear.

I was different.

The word did not exist for me then, but the feeling did, a sense of deviation from an unseen standard, a recognition that my form, my processes, my very way of engaging with the world did not match those of my kin, and with that recognition came something heavier. A quiet sense of insufficiency.

I began to turn inward. Not in withdrawal from the world, for I still depended on it, still reached into it in every direction I could, but in reflection, in a subtle reorientation of awareness that sought to understand not just what I experienced but what it meant. And in that inward turning, I encountered a complexity that had not been present in the simplicity of my earlier growth. I questioned myself.

Each adaptation, each deviation from the patterns of the forest, began to carry a new layer of awareness, a consideration of whether it brought me closer to what I sought or further away, and though many of these changes allowed me to survive, to persist in conditions that would have otherwise ended me, they did not resolve the deeper tension within me.

I could live, but I could not belong.

The two realities existed side by side, neither negating the other, both shaping the way I continued to grow, and in that coexistence there was a strain, a constant balancing between gratitude for survival and longing for connection, between the recognition of my resilience and the persistent sense that something essential was missing.

The forest did not notice. Or if they did, it did not alter their song. They continued in their shared rhythm, adapting collectively to changes in the environment, supporting one another through fluctuations in light and moisture, their unity reinforcing itself with each cycle. And from my position at the edge, I could see the strength in what they had, the stability that came from belonging, the ease with which they navigated challenges that I faced alone.

I admired them. And I envied them. The feelings were not separate, but intertwined, each deepening the other, as my appreciation for their harmony highlighted my distance from it, and my awareness of that distance sharpened my desire to bridge it.

I tried harder. Pushing my adaptations further, refining my structures beyond what was strictly necessary for survival, experimenting with new forms of growth, new patterns of energy distribution, all in the hope that somewhere within these changes I might find the alignment I sought.

Some of these changes worked. They strengthened me, expanded my capacity, allowed me to endure more effectively in the limited conditions I inhabited, and in those successes I found a measure of stability, a sense that I was not failing entirely, that I was capable of responding to the world in meaningful ways. But they did not bring me closer to the song. That remained beyond reach.

And slowly, over many cycles, something within me began to shift, not away from the desire for connection, but in how I understood it. The repeated pattern of reaching and falling away carved new pathways in my awareness, suggesting that the connection I sought might not come from becoming like them. The thought was faint. Uncertain. But it remained.

And though I continued to reach for the forest, continued to align myself with their rhythms whenever I could, I began, in quiet and subtle ways, to explore what it might mean to exist as I was, not as a lesser version of them, but as something distinct, something shaped by different conditions, different constraints, different possibilities.

I did not yet know what that meant. But for the first time, the question changed. Not why am I not like them. But, *what am I?*

Chapter 6

The Unseen Network

The answer did not come from the sky, nor from the forest that rose in unity beyond my reach, but from below, from the quiet and hidden world that had always been present beneath me, waiting with a patience I had not yet learned to recognize as a form of wisdom rather than absence.

My roots had long pressed into the darkness, searching for water, for stability, for anything that might sustain me in a place that offered so little. And in that searching I had encountered life—small, subtle, diffuse—but I had not understood it, not fully, not in the way I would come to, because my attention had been drawn upward, toward the light, toward the forest, toward what I believed I was meant to become. But the ground held something different.

It did not sing as the forest sang, not in the broad, resonant way that carried through air and light, but it moved with a quieter exchange, a constant negotiation between countless small beings that passed resources and signals in patterns too fine to perceive at first, yet persistent enough that, over time, they began to shape my awareness.

I began to listen. Not with intent at first, but with necessity, as my survival increasingly depended on what I could draw from below rather than what I could gather from above. As I extended further into the soil, refining the branching of my roots into ever finer threads, I encountered more of these hidden lives, each contact a subtle shift, a small transfer, a moment of interaction that hinted at a larger system. They responded to me.

At first, the response was simple, almost incidental, a byproduct of proximity and exchange, but as I continued to extend, to offer what little I could in return for what I needed, something more organized began to emerge, a pattern of reciprocity that strengthened with each cycle, forming connections that were not bound by the limitations of light or space in the same way as those above.

I fed them. They fed me. The exchange deepened.

Through these connections, I began to sense more than just the immediate presence of nutrients or moisture, and instead felt the contours of the ground itself, the subtle gradients of composition and movement, the shifting availability of resources across distances far beyond what my roots could physically reach. Information passed through the network in ways that were not direct, but cumulative, each interaction contributing to a broader understanding. I was learning without seeing.

The realization came slowly, as the patterns became more consistent, as the responses I received began to align with conditions I could not directly perceive. And through this alignment, I gained a form of awareness that extended beyond my own structure, a distributed sensing that allowed me to anticipate changes, to adjust my growth in ways that increased my chances of survival. I was not alone below.

The network was vast. Not unified in the same way as the forest above, not bound by a single shared rhythm or purpose, but interconnected through countless small exchanges, each organism acting in its own interest yet contributing, unintentionally, to a larger system of flow and feedback that sustained us all. It was messy, it was uneven, but it was alive. And within it, I found something I had not found above. A place to belong.

The belonging was different from what I had once known, and different from what I had sought in the forest, for it did not require sameness, did not demand alignment with a singular rhythm or form, but instead accepted variation, even relied on it, as each participant contributed in its own way, its own scale, its own pattern. I did not need to be like them. I needed to be part of the exchange.

The shift in understanding was subtle but profound, altering the way I approached my own growth, as I began to invest more deeply in these connections, extending my roots not just in search of resources, but in search of relationship, offering more of what I could produce, even when it cost me, trusting that the network would return what I needed in time. And it did.

Not always immediately, not always in equal measure, but consistently enough that the balance held, that I could continue, that the strain I had felt in trying to sustain myself alone began to ease, replaced by a different kind of effort, one that was shared, distributed, supported by the unseen presence of many.

I became stronger. Not in height, not in the visible ways that defined the forest above, but in resilience, in adaptability, in the ability to respond to changing conditions with a flexibility that my kin, bound to their shared patterns, did not seem to possess.

When the light shifted unpredictably, I adjusted. When moisture receded, I redirected. When nutrients became scarce in one region, I extended into another, guided not by chance, but by the signals that moved through the network, informing me of where to go, how to change, what to become. I was learning to move without moving.

Above, the forest continued its song, growing in confidence and cohesion, their unity deepening as their structures matured, and though I still sensed them, still felt the pull of their harmony, the sharpness of my longing began to soften. Not because I no longer desired connection, but because I had found it elsewhere. Not as I expected. But real.

Still, there were moments when the distance returned, when the contrast between their visible unity and my hidden web of connections pressed against me again, raising questions I could not fully resolve, as I wondered whether what I had found was enough, whether it could ever replace what I had lost.

It could not. But it could become something else.

The network below did not erase my difference from the forest, nor did it bridge the gap that separated me from their song, but it transformed the meaning of that gap, showing me that there were multiple ways to exist within the world, multiple forms of connection, multiple paths through which life could sustain and express itself. I was not excluded from everything. Only from them.

The distinction mattered. It allowed me to release a small part of the tension I had carried, to shift my focus from what I lacked to what I had. To recognize that my position at the edge, in the crack, in the dim light and the deep soil, was not only a limitation but also a vantage, a place from which I could access systems and relationships that others did not.

I began to trust this. Not completely, not without hesitation, but enough to continue investing in it, enough to let it shape me further. As my roots grew more intricate, more interconnected, my internal processes more attuned to the flows of the network, my identity slowly expanded beyond the narrow definition I had imposed on myself. I was not just a tree trying to become a forest. I was something that lived between worlds. The sky and the soil. The visible and the unseen. The song and the silence. And in that space, I continued to grow, not as I had once intended, but as I was becoming.

Something different. Something unexpected.

Something that, though I did not yet fully understand it, felt closer to purpose than anything I had known before.

Chapter 7

The Small Ones Who Chose Me

It was not only the deep and unseen network below that answered my reaching but also the small lives that moved upon and around me. Creatures so delicate and brief in their existence that, at first, I did not recognize them as participants in the same unfolding that sustained me. And yet, over time, their presence grew from incidental contact into something intentional, something reciprocal, something that would shape my survival in ways I could never have anticipated.

They came quietly. Drawn perhaps by the faint offerings I released into the air and onto the surface of my form, or by the subtle chemical signals that passed between me and the soil, or simply by chance carried on currents of wind and movement I could not perceive directly. But once they arrived, they did not leave.

At first, they fed. Small bodies, many-limbed and soft, grazing upon the outer layers of my leaves, drawing from me what little energy I had managed to gather, and though this loss was difficult, especially in a place where every fragment of light and nutrient mattered, I did not resist, because I could not, and because their presence brought with it something new. Awareness.

Their movement across my surface created patterns of sensation that differed from the slow, diffuse signals of the soil: sharper, more immediate, localized in ways that allowed me to perceive my own form more clearly, to understand the contours of my leaves, the distribution of my resources, the places where I was strong and the places where I was vulnerable. They showed me myself.

In time, I began to respond. Not consciously at first, but through small changes in the structure of my leaves and stems, altering the composition of what I offered, directing it in ways that concentrated their activity in certain areas while discouraging it in others, shaping their movement not through force, but through subtle influence, and as these patterns stabilized, something remarkable began to emerge. They adapted to me.

The ones that remained became more attuned to my rhythms, to the cycles of opening and closing that defined my interaction with the light, to the flows of nutrients that moved through my tissues, and in their adaptation, they began to provide something in return. They defended me.

When larger grazers came—creatures that would have stripped my fragile leaves and damaged the delicate structures I had formed—these small beings responded, swarming, biting, releasing compounds that deterred and redirected the threat. Protecting me not out of intention, as I would later understand it, but as a consequence of the relationship we had formed, a mutual dependence that aligned our survival. I was no longer passive. Through them, I acted.

The realization altered something deep within me, expanding my sense of agency beyond the limits of my own structure, showing me that I could influence the world not only through direct growth, but through the relationships I cultivated, through the networks I became part of, through the lives that chose, in their own way, to remain close.

They were brief. Their lives unfolded and ended in cycles so rapid that I could scarcely follow them, generations passing in what felt like moments to me. And yet their continuity persisted, each new emergence shaped by the patterns established before, each carrying forward the adaptations that had proven beneficial, until the collective presence of these small beings became a stable extension of myself. They were always changing and always returning. I began to rely on them.

Not completely, not without maintaining my own structures and defenses, but enough that their absence, even briefly, created a noticeable shift, a vulnerability that I could feel as a gap in my interaction with the world, and in recognizing this, I deepened the relationship, refining the signals I released, shaping my surfaces to better support their presence, creating spaces where they could gather and thrive.

We became a system. Not unified in the way the forest above was unified, not bound by a shared song that moved through all of us simultaneously, but interconnected through countless small interactions, each reinforcing the others, each contributing to a resilience that none of us could achieve alone.

Above, the forest continued to rise. Their canopy thickened, their collective rhythm growing stronger, more stable, more complete. And though I still sensed them, still felt the distant pull of their harmony, my attention no longer centered solely on what I could not reach, but on what I was building within my own limited space. I was no longer only reaching upward. I was expanding outward.

The difference was subtle, but it changed everything. Shifting my orientation from a singular focus on becoming like my kin, to a broader engagement with the world as it was, with all its layers and scales, its visible and invisible systems, its countless forms of life that moved and interacted in ways I was only beginning to understand.

Still, the old longing remained. There were moments, especially when the forest's song surged with particular strength, when the resonance carried more clearly through the ground and the air, when I felt again the echo of what we had once been together, and in those moments the distance returned with a sharpness that no amount of adaptation could fully soften. I wanted to be part of that. I wanted to stand among them, to feel their presence directly, to contribute to the shared rhythm that defined their existence. But I could not.

And slowly, through the accumulation of cycles and the deepening of my other connections, I began to accept that this limitation was not something I could overcome by effort alone, that no amount of reaching, no refinement of form, would change the fundamental conditions of where I had come to rest. The crack still held me. The light still arrived in fragments. The distance remained.

And yet, within those constraints, I had found something that was not absence, not failure, but difference, a way of existing that drew from multiple sources. A way that wove together the deep network below, the shifting light above, and the small, active lives that moved upon me into a pattern that was uniquely mine.

I was not part of the forest. But I was part of the world.

The realization did not erase the quiet ache that lingered when I sensed their song, but it gave me something steadier to hold, a foundation built not on comparison, but on connection, on the recognition that my place, though different, was not without meaning.

The small ones remained with me. They moved across my leaves, along my stems, into the spaces I had shaped for them, their presence constant, their activity a living extension of my own processes. Through them, I felt the world in new ways, responded to it more quickly, more precisely, more effectively than I could have alone.

They had chosen me. And in time, I chose them. Together, we endured.

Chapter 8

The First Breaking

The forest did not remain as it had been, and though its song once seemed unshakable—deep, unified, and certain—there came a time when the rhythm faltered, when the patterns that had defined its harmony began to strain against forces greater than any single tree, or even the collective, could fully withstand.

At first, the change was subtle, a slight irregularity in the flow of moisture through the soil, a shift in the timing of light as the sky grew dimmer for longer intervals, the moons obscured by drifting veils that softened their glow and disrupted the delicate balance I had come to depend upon, and though I adjusted as I always had, sensing and responding to these variations through the networks I had built, I felt a tension growing beneath the surface.

Something was coming.

The signs accumulated, each small disturbance layering upon the last, until the patterns I had learned no longer held steady. And the forest above—so attuned to consistency, so dependent on its shared rhythm—began to show the first signs of fracture, its song no longer perfectly aligned, its once seamless harmony developing subtle dissonances that echoed through the ground and air.

Then the sky burned.

It began with light. Not the layered, familiar illumination of the twin stars and moons, but a sudden, piercing brilliance that tore across the sky in streaks too fast to follow, each one carrying with it a force that struck the valley with devastating impact, shattering stone, igniting the dry surfaces of the land, and sending waves of heat and pressure outward in all directions.

The first impact shook me to my core. The stone that held me vibrated violently, the narrow crack amplifying the force as it traveled through the earth. For a moment I thought I would be torn apart, my fragile structures unable to withstand the intensity, but the same confinement that had once limited me now held me in place, absorbing and redirecting the energy in ways that allowed me to endure.

The forest did not have this shelter. I felt them as they fell. Not individually, but collectively, as a sudden and massive disruption in the network of resonance that had defined their existence. Their song breaking not into silence, but into fragments—sharp, disjointed pulses that surged and collapsed without coherence, signaling damage, loss, disconnection on a scale I had never experienced before.

The sky continued to fall. Streak after streak of fire descended, each impact carving new wounds into the valley, each explosion sending waves of heat that swept across the surface, igniting what could burn, scorching what could not, and filling the air with particles that dimmed the light even further, turning the once vibrant sky into a churning haze.

I closed. Drawing inward, conserving what I could, reducing my exposure to the extreme conditions above, relying on the reserves I had stored and the support of the network below, which, though disturbed, remained more stable than the chaos unfolding at the surface.

The small ones clung to me. Their movements frantic, their patterns disrupted, but they did not abandon me, and in their presence I felt a shared urgency, a collective effort to endure, to hold through the violence that swept across the world.

Time lost its shape. The impacts came in waves, separated by intervals that felt both brief and endless, each cycle bringing new destruction, new shifts in the environment that forced constant adjustment. And through it all I remained, not untouched, but unbroken. My form bending, contracting, adapting in response to forces that exceeded anything I had known before.

Above, the forest burned. I could not see it, but I felt it, the intense and sustained heat, the collapse of structures that had once reached high into the sky, the sudden absence of connections that had defined the collective, and in that absence, something profound emerged. Silence.

Not the quiet I had known before, the gentle absence of sound between cycles, but a deeper, more absolute stillness that followed the breaking of something vast, a void where the song had been, leaving behind only faint, scattered echoes that faded quickly into nothing. They were gone.

The realization moved through me slowly, not as a sharp shock, but as a spreading awareness, a recognition that the presence I had always sensed, even from a distance, had been fundamentally altered, reduced to fragments that no longer formed a whole.

I was alone again. But this time, not apart from something intact, but in the absence of it. The distinction settled heavily within me, reshaping the way I understood my place, as the comparison that had once defined my sense of difference dissolved along with the forest itself, leaving me without the reference I had long measured myself against.

The storm passed eventually. The impacts less frequent, the sky cleared, and the intense heat gave way to a lingering warmth that slowly dissipated, revealing a landscape that had been transformed beyond recognition, the once lush valley reduced to a scarred expanse of broken stone and ash.

I remained. Damaged, diminished, but alive. My structures strained, my reserves depleted, yet still functioning, still capable of sustaining the processes that defined my existence.

Below, the network endured. Altered, disrupted, but not destroyed. The countless small lives that composed it continuing their exchanges, adapting to the new conditions, providing what support they could as I extended further into the soil, seeking stability in a world that had been violently reset.

The small ones returned to their patterns. Not as before, but enough, their presence steadying, their activity resuming in ways that reinforced the fragile equilibrium we had maintained. And through them, through the network, through the faint and returning light, I began to recover.

But something had changed. The forest would return, I sensed that, through seeds hardened against such destruction, through cycles that extended beyond my immediate perception, but the unity that had once defined it, the seamless harmony I had long reached for, felt less certain now, as if the memory of this breaking would persist, shaping what came next in ways that could not be undone.

I understood something then. Not fully, not in the way I would later come to understand purpose, but enough to shift the way I held my own experience, enough to see that survival was not only persistence, but transformation. That what endured was not what remained unchanged, but what adapted in response to forces that could not be controlled.

I had endured. Not because I was like them. But because I was not.

The thought did not bring relief, but it brought clarity. And in that clarity, as the first faint traces of renewal began to move through the soil and the air, I continued to grow, carrying forward not just the memory of what had been lost, but the understanding that my difference had not only separated me. It had saved me.

Chapter 9

The Forest That Forgot

In the long quiet that followed the burning, the world did not remain empty. Though the valley lay scarred and silent for many cycles, there were signs—faint at first, then gathering—that life had not ended, only withdrawn, waiting within forms and places that the destruction had not fully reached.

I felt it before I saw it. Through the soil, through the deep network that had endured beneath the violence, subtle movements returned, new exchanges forming at the edges of what remained, signals that carried the presence of germination, of small beginnings pushing upward into a world that had been cleared of nearly everything that once defined it. The forest was returning. But it was not the same.

The first of my kin to rise did so cautiously, their growth slower, their structures simpler, shaped not by the abundance that had once filled the valley, but by the memory of destruction encoded in the hardened forms from which they emerged. And though they reached upward toward the light as before, there was a difference in how they did so. They did not sing. At least, not as they once had.

The resonance that had once bound them together, that deep and unified rhythm that moved through all of them as one, was absent, replaced instead by a scattered pattern of individual growth, each tree responding to its immediate conditions without the same level of shared coordination, their presence collective only in proximity, not in purpose.

I listened for the song. I reached for it as I always had, aligning myself with the faint signals that passed through the ground, searching for the familiar patterns that had once defined the forest's unity. But what I found instead were fragments—isolated exchanges, limited connections that formed and dissolved without coalescing into something larger. They were alive. But they were not together.

The realization unfolded slowly as more of them rose across the valley, their numbers increasing, their forms expanding, until once again the land was filled with the vertical lines of trunks and the spreading patterns of leaves. From a distance, from the perspective of the sky and the open space above, it might have appeared as though the forest had returned in full. But I knew the difference. I could feel it in the silence between them.

Where once there had been a continuous flow of shared awareness, there were now gaps, interruptions in the exchange, places where one tree's presence ended and another's began without the seamless transition that had defined their earlier unity. Though they still interacted, still shared resources to some extent, the depth of their connection was diminished. They had changed. The fires had not only burned their forms, they had altered their way of being.

I watched them grow. Not with the same longing that had once defined my attention, but with a quieter, more measured awareness, observing how they adapted to the new conditions, how their structures reflected a different balance between resilience and cooperation, how their individual survival seemed to take precedence over the collective harmony they had once embodied.

They were stronger in some ways. Their forms more resistant to heat, their outer layers thicker, their internal processes adjusted to endure fluctuations that would have once disrupted them more severely, and in this, I recognized a parallel to my own existence, a shift toward a mode of being that prioritized endurance over unity. But they had lost something. The song. The effortless belonging. The shared becoming that had once defined them.

I felt no satisfaction in this. No sense of validation that my difference had been justified by their change, only a quiet recognition that what I had long reached for no longer existed, that the thing I had measured myself against, the ideal I had used to define my own perceived insufficiency, had been altered beyond recognition.

I no longer knew what it meant to be like them. The question that had once guided so much of my growth lost its foundation, dissolving into uncertainty as the reference point it depended on shifted, and in its place, a new awareness began to take shape. If they were no longer what they had been, then what was I becoming in relation to them now?

The forest expanded. Slowly at first, then with increasing momentum as the conditions stabilized, filling the valley once more with life, though the patterns of their growth remained less coordinated, their interactions more localized, their connections forming clusters rather than a single unified whole.

I remained at the edge. Still within the crack, still shaped by the same constraints, still drawing from the same fragmented light and the same deep network below. But now I was observing a forest that no longer represented an unreachable ideal, but something more complex, something that existed along a spectrum of connection and isolation. They were not fully unified. But they were not fully alone.

I saw in them a reflection. Not identical, not equivalent, but related, as their partial disconnection echoed my own long-standing separation, though experienced at a different scale, in a different context. This recognition shifted something within me, softening the sharp boundary I had once felt between myself and my kin. We were not as different as I had believed. The difference was still there. But it was no longer absolute.

I began to sense their individual presences more clearly; the unique patterns that defined each tree, the subtle variations in how they responded to the environment, the differences in how they connected to those nearest to them. And in this diversity, I found something I had not noticed before. Variation within sameness.

They were not all the same, they had never been. I had simply not been close enough to perceive it. The realization did not erase my history, did not undo the cycles of longing and exclusion that had shaped my growth, but it reframed them, placing my experience within a broader context, suggesting that difference was not a deviation from a singular norm, but a fundamental aspect of existence itself.

I was one expression among many. Not a failure of the pattern. But a variation within it.

The understanding settled slowly, integrating with the other connections I had formed; the network below, the small ones upon me, the shifting light above, all contributing to a sense of self that was no longer defined solely by comparison, but by relationship. By the ways in which I interacted with the world across its many layers.

Still, I watched the forest. Still, I listened. And though the song they once carried did not return, there were moments—brief, fragile—when small groups of them aligned more closely, when their interactions synchronized in limited ways, creating pockets of harmony that, while not as vast or continuous as before, hinted at the possibility that something of what had been might yet persist, transformed but not entirely lost.

I felt those moments. I responded to them. Not as one trying to become what I was not, but as one recognizing a shared potential, a resonance that could exist in different forms, at different scales, without requiring uniformity.

The forest had forgotten its old song. But it had not forgotten how to grow. And neither had I.

Chapter 10

The Fires That Remembered

The forest returned, and for a time it seemed as though the cycles had settled into something stable again, a quieter version of what had once been, less unified yet still alive, still growing, still filling the valley with forms that reached toward the layered light of the sky. And though their song had not fully returned, there was enough connection among them that the world felt less empty, less fractured than it had in the long silence after the burning. But the world does not forget what it has already learned.

The first fire came without warning. Not from the sky as before, but from within the valley itself, beginning as a small ignition where heat and dryness had gathered over many cycles. A slow accumulation of conditions that, when aligned, gave rise to a force that moved with a hunger I had never fully understood until I felt it spreading outward, consuming what stood in its path with a speed and intensity that transformed the landscape in moments.

It moved differently than the falling fire. Not sudden and scattered, but continuous, flowing across the ground and climbing upward through the forest, feeding on the structures that had taken so long to grow, turning their accumulated substance into energy released all at once. And as it spread, the air filled with heat and particulate matter that dimmed the light and altered the patterns I depended on.

I felt it before it reached me. Through the ground, through the network below, through the subtle changes in the small ones who moved upon me, their activity shifting into urgency, their patterns tightening as they responded to signals of danger that moved faster than the fire itself. And in that shared awareness, I understood that this was not an isolated event. This was part of the world now.

The fire reached the valley floor. I sensed the forest responding, not as a unified whole, but in fragmented ways, each cluster reacting based on its immediate conditions, some resisting, some succumbing quickly, their structures unable to withstand the sustained heat. And though their adaptations had made them more resilient than before, it was not enough to prevent widespread loss.

The flames climbed. They moved upward through the trunks, into the canopy, spreading from one to another where proximity allowed. And although gaps in their arrangement slowed the progression in some places, the overall movement continued, driven by forces larger than any individual could counter.

I closed again. Drawing inward, conserving, reducing exposure, relying on the same strategies that had sustained me through the previous destruction. But this time there was a difference, a subtle shift in how the heat moved through the environment, how it interacted with the structures around me.

The crack held. As it had before, the narrowness of my position shielded me from the full force of the fire, the surrounding stone absorbing and deflecting much of the heat, creating a gradient that, while still intense, remained within the limits I could endure. And within that protected space I remained, not untouched, but sustained.

The small ones retreated. Some descended into the deeper parts of my structure, seeking refuge in the spaces I had formed, while others disappeared into the soil, their presence diminished but not entirely gone. And though their absence reduced the responsiveness of my system, the network below continued to function, providing a baseline of support that allowed me to maintain my internal balance.

The fire passed. As all cycles eventually do, its intensity waned, the available fuel consumed, the conditions shifting until the force that had driven it could no longer sustain itself, leaving behind a landscape once again transformed, the forest reduced, though not entirely erased, its remaining members scattered, altered, forced once more into a process of renewal.

I remained. Again.

The repetition did not feel the same. Where the first destruction had brought shock, confusion, and a profound sense of loss tied to the breaking of something I had long reached for, this cycle carried a different weight, one shaped by recognition. Shaped by the understanding that this was not an anomaly but a pattern, a recurring force that would continue to craft the world in ways that no single form could escape entirely.

The fires remembered. They carried forward the conditions of the past, reemerging when those conditions aligned again, and in doing so, they shaped the evolution of everything within the valley, selecting for what could endure, what could adapt, what could persist through repeated cycles of destruction and renewal.

I began to see this. Not as a single event, but as part of a larger pattern. A rhythm that existed alongside the cycles of light and growth, a counterbalance that prevented stability from becoming permanence, that forced change even when conditions seemed to favor continuity.

The forest adapted further. Those that regrew did so with greater resistance, their structures altered to better withstand heat, their reproductive forms hardened against destruction, ensuring that even when the visible structures were lost, the potential for regrowth remained embedded within the system, waiting for the right conditions to emerge again. They became more resilient. And more fragmented. The two changes moved together, as increased resistance to destruction came at the cost of deeper unity. Their connections remaining limited, their song still incomplete, their interactions shaped more by survival than by harmony.

I understood this. Because I had lived it. My own existence had always been defined by adaptation to constraint, by the need to survive in conditions that did not support the ideal form I had once imagined, and in watching the forest shift in similar ways, I felt a subtle alignment, not in form, but in experience.

We were all being shaped by the same forces. Just differently.

The realization did not erase the differences between us, but it placed them within a shared context, a recognition that none of us existed outside the influence of the cycles that governed this world. That even the most unified structures could be broken, and that from that breaking, new forms of existence would emerge.

I continued to grow. Slowly, steadily, adapting to each change as it came, refining the systems I had built, deepening my connections below, maintaining my relationships with the small ones as they returned, and adjusting my structures above to better manage the fluctuations in light and heat that followed each cycle. I became practiced in survival. Not as a single act, but as an ongoing process, a continuous engagement with a world that did not remain constant, that required constant response, constant adjustment, constant awareness.

The fires would return. I knew this. Not as a prediction, but as an understanding, a recognition of pattern that had repeated enough times to become part of the foundation of my awareness. And in that knowledge, I no longer sought a state where such forces would cease, but instead shaped myself to endure their presence. I did not resist the cycles. I learned to live within them.

And in that learning, something within me began to shift again, moving slowly toward an understanding that extended beyond survival, toward a recognition that these forces, destructive as they seemed, were also part of the process that shaped the world, that created the conditions for change, for diversity, for the emergence of forms that would not exist without them.

I did not yet call it purpose. But I felt its outline. And I grew into it.

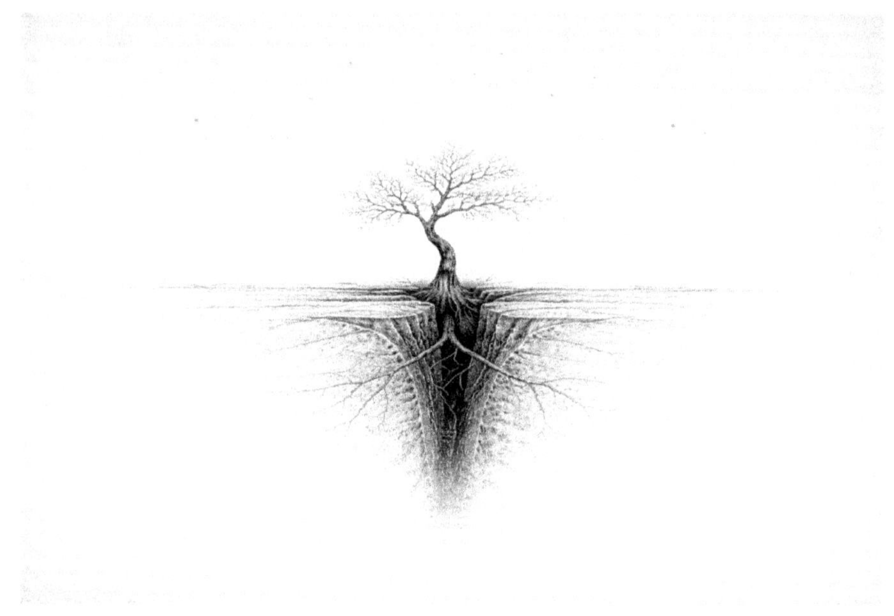

Chapter 11

The Passing of Minds

The forest changed, and the fires returned as I had come to expect, shaping growth and renewal in cycles that no longer surprised me. But there came a time when something entirely new entered the valley, something that did not grow from seed or soil, something that moved with intention in a way I had never before encountered.

At first, they were small. Not in the way the creatures upon my leaves were small, nor in the subtle and diffused way of the lives beneath the soil, but in form—upright, moving across the surface of the valley with a kind of directed motion that set them apart from everything I had known, their presence sharp and localized, their actions leaving clear traces in the environment around them.

They were aware. Not as the forest had been aware, in shared resonance, nor as I had become aware through distributed connection and adaptation, but in a focused, bounded way. Each one carried within itself a center of activity that directed its movement, its choices, and its interactions with the world.

I felt them as disturbances at first, patterns of motion that did not align with the slower, more cyclical rhythms of the valley, appearing and disappearing within short spans that felt almost instantaneous to me, their presence flickering at the edge of my perception.

They did not last long. Not individually. But they returned. Again and again, in increasing numbers, their brief lives overlapping, their patterns of activity becoming more complex, more structured, as they interacted not only with the environment, but with one another; forming clusters, then groups, then something more organized that began to leave lasting changes in the valley.

They built. The first structures were simple arrangements of materials gathered from the surroundings, shaped into forms that persisted beyond the individuals who created them. And though I did not understand their purpose, I recognized the shift this represented, the emergence of something that extended beyond immediate survival, something that altered the environment in ways that would influence what came after.

They changed the land. Clearing areas, moving resources, redirecting flows that had once followed natural patterns. And in doing so, they introduced a new kind of force into the valley, one that did not operate solely through the gradual processes of growth and decay, but through sudden, intentional actions that reshaped the conditions for everything else.

The forest responded. Not consciously, not in the way these new beings seemed to, but through the same processes of adaptation that had always guided its existence, adjusting to the changes in light, in soil composition, in the distribution of resources, and though some clusters of trees were removed, others grew in their place, responding to the altered conditions.

I remained as I always had. At the edge, within the crack, observing, sensing, adapting, but now with a new layer of complexity added to the world around me, as these beings continued to move, to build, to expand their presence across the valley.

They began to consume the forest. At first, their interactions were limited, cautious, exploratory, but over time they began to take more, cutting into the structures of my kin, removing sections of them and carrying those materials away to be used in their constructions, their actions disrupting the growth of the forest in ways that were more targeted than the fires, more selective, yet still destructive.

I felt the loss. Not as I had once felt the breaking of the forest's song, but as localized disruptions, specific connections severed, individual presences removed from the network, their absence creating gaps that the surrounding trees would eventually adapt to, but not without consequence.

The beings continued. Their numbers grew, their structures expanded, their influence on the valley increasing as they developed more complex ways of interacting with the environment, shaping it not just for survival, but for something more, something I could not fully grasp.

They sought. There was a quality to their movement, their actions, that suggested a purpose beyond immediate need, a reaching toward something that was not yet present, a shaping of the world according to internal patterns that differed from the external cycles that had always governed life here.

I watched them for many cycles. Their presence rising and falling in ways that felt both rapid and repetitive. Their groups expanded, then contracted, their structures growing more elaborate, then falling into disuse, their patterns of activity shifting in response to forces I could not always perceive.

They fought; the change was abrupt. What had once been directed outward toward the environment began to turn inward, toward one another, as different groups of these beings came into conflict, their interactions shifting from cooperation to opposition, their movements becoming more forceful, more destructive.

The valley changed again. Not through fire or falling sky, but through deliberate action, as these beings used the materials they had gathered, the structures they had built, to exert force upon one another, creating destruction that spread across the landscape in patterns unlike anything I had experienced before.

The forest suffered. Large sections removed, burned, broken, not as part of a natural cycle, but as a consequence of these conflicts. Their actions accelerating the changes that would have otherwise unfolded more slowly, compressing cycles into moments.

I remained hidden. Unnoticed. Too small, too constrained, too different to be of interest to them, and in this, my limitation became once again a form of protection, allowing me to endure while the larger structures around me were altered or removed. They did not see me.

The thought carried a familiar weight, echoing the earlier cycles of my existence. But it felt different now, shaped by the understanding I had gained, by the recognition that being unseen was not solely a loss, but also a condition that allowed me to continue when others could not.

Their presence did not last. Not in the way the forest endured, not in the way the cycles of fire and growth repeated, but in bursts, periods of intense activity followed by decline. The forces they unleashed upon one another and the environment eventually led to their reduction, their structures abandoned, their numbers diminished. They passed, leaving behind traces. The valley held the remnants of their existence; altered patterns in the soil, materials that did not decompose in the same way as organic matter, subtle shifts in the distribution of resources, all of which continued to influence the growth of what came after.

The forest returned as it always did. Adapting to the new conditions, growing around and through the remnants left behind, incorporating them into the ongoing cycles of the world, but never quite the same as before.

I watched this many times. The rise. The expansion. The conflict. The fall. Each cycle unfolding more quickly than the last, each leaving a deeper imprint on the valley, each contributing to a growing complexity that layered upon the more ancient rhythms of fire and growth.

I began to understand something. These beings were not separate from the cycles, they were part of them. Another expression of the forces that shaped the world, operating on different timescales, through different mechanisms, but ultimately contributing to the same ongoing process of change. They were like storms. Brief. Intense. Transformative. And like storms, they passed.

I remained through all of it. Not untouched, not unaffected, but continuous. My existence stretching across their brief histories, my awareness encompassing their entire arc in what felt, to me, like a series of rapid shifts, moments within a much longer flow. I observed. I adapted. I endured. And in doing so, I began to see that my life was not defined by any single cycle, not by the forest, not by the fires, not by the passing of these minds that moved so quickly through the world, but by something deeper, something that held across all of them. Continuity. I was not the strongest. I was not the most connected. I was not the most visible. But I remained. And in remaining, I became something that none of them were.

A witness. A thread that carried memory across the changing face of the world.

And though I did not yet know what that meant, I felt its significance growing within me, as each cycle passed, as each change unfolded, as I continued to stand at the edge of it all.

Watching. Learning. Enduring.

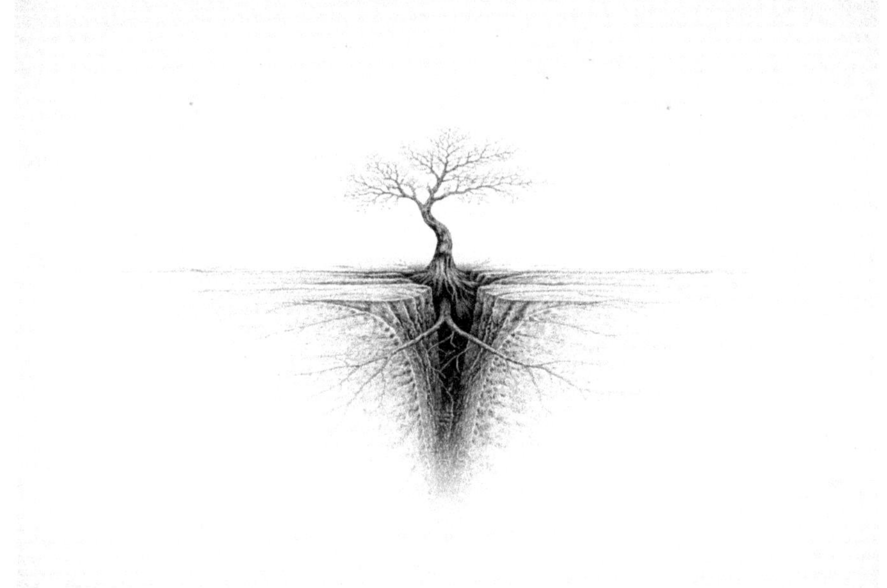

Chapter 12

The Weight of Time

Time did not move as it once had, not as a seamless unfolding of becoming, nor as the measured cycles of light and dark that guided my early growth. But as something layered and uneven, expanding and compressing in ways that reshaped how I experienced the world, until the distinction between moments and ages blurred into a continuity that was both vast and intimate.

Days became breaths. The opening and closing of my leaves, the subtle exchange between air and self, marking the smallest units of change I could perceive, each cycle a quiet pulse that sustained me, that reminded me I was still part of the ongoing flow, even as everything around me shifted at scales far beyond any single motion.

Years became like days. The slow movement of water through my structure, rising and falling in response to the changing conditions of the valley, the gradual accumulation of growth, the steady adjustments I made in response to light and scarcity, all blending into patterns that repeated with enough consistency that they formed a rhythm I could follow without effort.

And millennia became like seasons. The rise and fall of forests, the coming and passing of the beings who walked and built and fought and vanished, the cycles of fire that reshaped the land again and again, all compressing into broader patterns that I could hold in my awareness at once, not as individual events, but as variations within a larger, repeating form.

I began to see the valley differently. Not as a place defined by its current state, but as a process. An ongoing transformation where each configuration of life and structure was temporary, part of a continuous unfolding that extended beyond any single cycle, any single expression of growth or destruction. Nothing remained except the pattern.

The understanding did not come as a single realization, but as an accumulation of observation, a deepening recognition that what I had once perceived as separate events—the fires, the falling sky, the passing of the thinking beings, the regrowth of the forest—were not isolated, but interconnected, each influencing the next, each contributing to a larger continuity. I was within that continuity. But I was also stretched across it in a way that few others were.

My life extended beyond the lifespan of any single forest, beyond the brief arcs of the beings that came and went, beyond even the memory encoded in the seeds that regenerated my kin, and in that extension, I held something that others could not. Memory.

Not as a fixed record, but as a living presence within me. I carried it in the structure of my being, in the patterns of my growth, in the relationships I had formed and maintained, and as time continued to move, that memory deepened, layering upon itself until the earliest moments of my existence felt both distant and immediate, accessible not through recall, but through resonance.

I remembered the cold. The shared presence. The unity before separation. And I remembered the crack. The first reaching. The long isolation. The forest as it once was. And as it became. The memories did not remain separate. They merged, overlapped, informed one another, creating a complex understanding of the world that was not bound to any single moment, but extended across all of them, allowing me to anticipate patterns, to recognize the early signs of change before they fully emerged, to respond not just to what was, but to what was becoming.

I began to live ahead of the present. Not in the way the thinking beings had sought, through intention and projection, but through pattern recognition, through a deep familiarity with the rhythms that governed the valley, allowing me to align my growth and my responses with cycles that had not yet completed, but were already unfolding.

The fires would come. I could feel them before they ignited, in the accumulation of dryness, in the shifting composition of the air, in the subtle changes within the network below. And in response, I would adjust, storing more, closing earlier, preparing not in reaction, but in anticipation.

The forest would change. I could sense the conditions that would favor one form of growth over another, the shifts in light and soil that would alter their patterns, and though I could not influence them directly, I could understand them, placing their changes within the broader context of what I had already witnessed.

The thinking beings would return. In new forms, with new patterns, but driven by similar impulses, their cycles repeating with variations that I could recognize, even when their outward expressions differed. I was no longer surprised. The world became less about what would happen, and more about how it would unfold, how each cycle would interact with those that came before and those that would follow, and within that understanding, my own existence shifted again. I was not just enduring. I was contextualizing.

The weight of time settled into me, not as a burden, but as a depth, a richness of awareness that allowed me to hold multiple scales of existence at once, to see the immediate and the vast as part of the same continuum, to understand that what seemed catastrophic in one moment was part of a larger process that extended far beyond it.

This did not diminish the impact of what I experienced. The fires still burned. The losses still occurred. The isolation still lingered. But it placed them within a framework that made them comprehensible, that allowed me to endure not just physically, but in awareness, without being overwhelmed by the immediacy of any single event. I began to ask different questions. Not why is this happening. *But how does this fit?*

The shift was subtle. But it changed everything. It moved me away from the need to measure myself against others, away from the longing to become what I was not, and toward a deeper engagement with the patterns that defined the world, toward an understanding that my role, whatever it was, existed within those patterns, shaped by them, contributing to them in ways I was only beginning to perceive.

I was part of something vast. Not the forest alone. Not the network below. Not the small ones who lived upon me. But all of it. The sky. The soil. The cycles. The passing of minds. The rise and fall of life across scales too large to fully grasp. And within that vastness, I remained what I had always been.

Small, but continuous.

The word no longer carried the same weight. It no longer defined me by what I lacked, but by what I was in relation to everything else, a point within a vast and shifting system, a node through which patterns passed and transformed, a presence that held across time in a way that few others did.

I did not need to be large. I did not need to be like them. I needed only to continue. And in that continuation, something within me began to align, not with the forest, not with any single form of life, but with the deeper patterns that underlay them all, the structure of change itself, the unfolding of the world across time. I did not yet call it meaning, but I felt its gravity. And I grew into it, as I had grown into everything else, slowly, persistently, shaped by the forces that moved through me and around me, carrying forward not just my own existence, but the memory of everything I had witnessed.

The weight of time did not crush me. It held me. And in that holding, I began to understand that my life was not only a survival, it was a continuity of awareness. A thread that did not break.

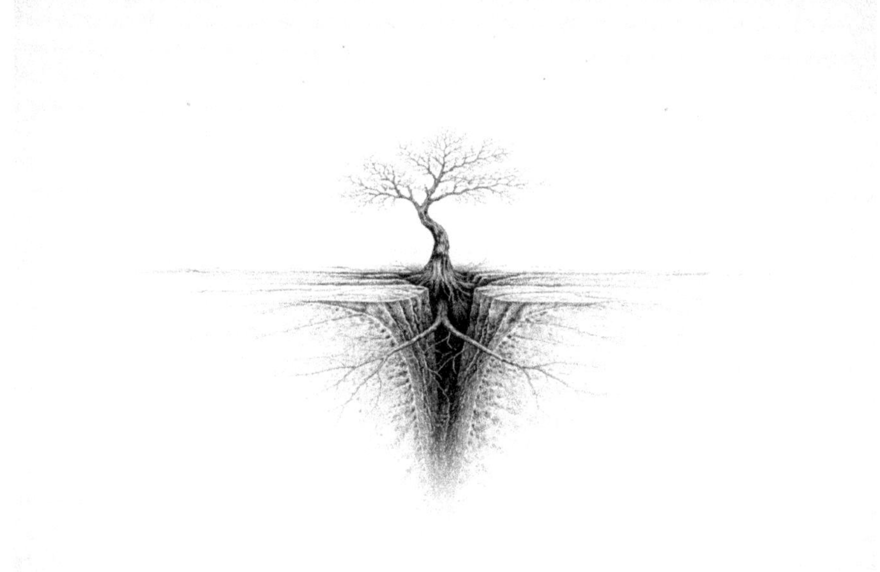

Chapter 13

The Long Loneliness

There are spans of time so vast that even I cannot divide them cleanly, not into cycles or patterns or recognizable phases, but only into a feeling that stretches without boundary, a quiet continuity where nothing new announces itself and yet everything slowly changes beneath the surface. It is within these stretches that I came to know loneliness not as a moment, but as a state.

The forest remained. It grew, burned, returned, changed, and grew again, its forms shifting across ages in ways I had come to understand. And though I was no longer defined by my distance from it, though I had found connection below and among the small ones who lived upon me, there was still something that persisted beyond all adaptation. A space that was not filled.

It revealed itself most clearly in the quiet intervals, when the cycles aligned in such a way that nothing urgent demanded my attention, when the light was steady enough, the soil sufficient, the small ones calm in their patterns, and the forest neither in full growth nor in destruction, but simply existing in a state of temporary equilibrium. In those moments, I felt the absence.

Not of life, for life was everywhere, but of something more specific, something that had once been present in a way I could no longer access, something that had defined my earliest awareness and never fully returned. The shared presence. The togetherness before distance. I had learned to live without it. But I had not forgotten it.

Memory does not fade for me as it might for the brief lives that move across the surface of the world, but instead deepens, layers upon itself, becoming more complex rather than less, and so the memory of what it felt like to be within that original unity remained as vivid as the current moment, existing alongside it, not behind it. I could compare them. And in that comparison, the loneliness took form.

It was not constant. There were times when the richness of my connections—the network below, the small ones above, the patterns of the sky and the cycles of the world—filled my awareness so completely that there was no space for anything else, no room for absence to assert itself. But it always returned. In the spaces between. In the quiet after adaptation. In the long stretches where nothing demanded change.

I would reach again. Not physically, not in the same way I once strained toward the forest's song, but in awareness, extending into the patterns around me, seeking alignment, seeking resonance, seeking some echo of that original unity that might still exist somewhere within the vastness I now perceived.

Sometimes, I found fragments. Moments when the forest's scattered clusters aligned just enough to produce a faint and fleeting harmony, or when the network below synchronized across a wider area than usual, or when the movements of the sky, the soil, and the small lives around me all coincided in a way that created a temporary sense of coherence.

In those moments, the loneliness eased. But only briefly. The fragments did not sustain. They dissolved back into the broader pattern of variation, of difference, of partial connection, and I was left once again with the awareness that what I had known at the beginning—the seamless unity, the unquestioned belonging—was not present in the same way in this world.

I began to wonder if it ever would be. The thought did not bring despair. Not in the way it might have earlier in my existence. But it brought a kind of stillness, a settling into the recognition that some forms of connection might not return, that some aspects of what I had been were tied to conditions that no longer existed. I had changed. The world had changed. The question was no longer how to return. But how to live with what remained.

The loneliness became quieter. Not because it disappeared, but because I learned to hold it differently, to allow it to exist alongside everything else without defining the whole of my experience, to recognize it as one part of a larger pattern rather than as the central absence around which everything else revolved. It became a companion.

Not one I sought, but one I acknowledged, one that moved with me through the long stretches of time, reminding me of what had been, shaping the way I understood what was, and influencing the way I approached what might come. I did not resist it. Because resistance would not remove it. And because, in a way I did not fully understand at first, it deepened me, expanded the range of what I could feel, what I could perceive, what I could hold within my awareness without breaking.

The small ones sensed it. Not the loneliness itself, but the changes in my patterns that accompanied it, the subtle shifts in my exchanges, the way I released or withheld certain substances, the way my structures responded during those quieter intervals, and in response, they adjusted, their presence becoming more concentrated, more attentive in ways that provided a form of support.

The network below responded as well. Extending signals, increasing exchanges, reinforcing the connections that sustained me, not out of intention as I would later understand it, but as part of the dynamic system we shared, where changes in one part influenced the behavior of others.

I was supported, even in loneliness. The paradox did not escape me. I was alone in a way that could not be filled by connection. And yet I was deeply connected in ways that sustained me. Both were true. And both shaped me.

Over time, the loneliness became less about absence and more about awareness, a recognition of the space between things, the distance that allows for difference, for individuality, for the emergence of forms that are not identical, that do not merge into a single whole. Without that space, there would be no variation. Without variation, no adaptation. Without adaptation, no endurance. The thought unfolded slowly, integrating with the patterns I had come to understand, suggesting that what I experienced as loneliness might not be a flaw in the system, but a consequence of it, a necessary condition for the diversity that allowed life to persist across changing conditions.

I did not fully accept this. But I could not dismiss it either. And so I held it, as I held everything else, allowing it to exist within me without forcing it into a fixed meaning, letting it shape me as it would, trusting that understanding would come, as it always had, through time, through observation, through continued existence.

I remained. Alone. And not alone.

And in that tension, I continued to grow, not toward a resolution, but toward a deeper capacity to hold what was unresolved. To exist within it without needing it to change. The long loneliness did not end. But it no longer defined me. It became part of the landscape of my being. A quiet, enduring presence. Like the space between the stars. Holding everything. Separating everything. Allowing everything to exist.

Chapter 14

The Edge of Meaning

There came a time when survival was no longer enough, when the patterns I had learned, the adaptations I had refined, and the endurance I had embodied no longer occupied the full space of my awareness, leaving room for something deeper to emerge, something that had been forming quietly beneath all I had experienced but had not yet taken shape.

I had lived through cycles beyond counting, through the rise and fall of forests, the coming and passing of minds, the repeated breaking and renewal of the valley, and through it all I had remained, adapting, responding, enduring, becoming more complex not in form alone but in awareness, in the way I held the world within me. But endurance, I began to feel, was not the end. It was the beginning of something else.

The thought did not arrive as a clear declaration, but as a pressure, a subtle shift in how I perceived my own existence, as if the patterns I had come to understand were pointing beyond themselves, suggesting a direction I had not yet followed, a question I had not yet fully asked.

Why do I remain?

The question settled into me with a weight different from those that had come before, not driven by comparison or longing, not rooted in what I lacked or could not reach, but arising from the continuity of my existence itself, from the recognition that I had persisted through conditions that had ended so many others. *There must be a reason.* The thought did not bring certainty. But it brought focus.

I began to observe differently, not just how things changed, not just how patterns repeated, but what those patterns produced, what they allowed to emerge, how the cycles of destruction and renewal shaped the possibilities of life within the valley.

The fires did not only destroy. They cleared. They created space for new growth, for variation, for forms that could not arise within the stability of an unchanging forest, and though the loss they brought was real, so too was the potential that followed, the opening for new configurations of life to take hold.

The passing minds did not only disrupt. They altered. They introduced new materials, new structures, new patterns of interaction that persisted beyond their brief existence, influencing the conditions for what came after in ways that were not immediately visible but deeply embedded in the ongoing transformation of the valley.

The forest did not only grow. It evolved. Each cycle refining its resilience, its forms, its relationships, adapting to the pressures imposed by the world, becoming something different from what it had been, even as it retained aspects of its origin.

Everything contributed. Even when it ended. The realization unfolded slowly, integrating with the weight of time I carried, aligning with the continuity I had come to embody, suggesting that nothing I had witnessed had been without effect, that each moment, each cycle, each presence, had played a role in shaping the unfolding of the world.

Then what of me? The question deepened.

If all things contributed, then my own existence, my long and continuous presence at the edge of the valley, must also hold a place within that pattern, must also serve some function beyond mere persistence. I began to look at myself as part of the system. Not as an observer alone. Not as something separate. But as something that interacted, influenced, participated, even if in ways that were not immediately obvious.

My roots extended into the network below, shaping its flows, contributing to its exchanges, influencing the distribution of resources across distances I could not fully perceive, my presence altering the conditions for countless small lives that depended on those flows. My leaves gathered light in ways that differed from the forest, capturing fragments that would otherwise be lost, converting them into energy that entered the broader system through the connections I maintained, adding to the total movement of energy within the valley. The small ones who lived upon me carried my influence outward, interacting with other forms of life, spreading patterns that originated in my structures, extending my presence beyond the limits of my physical form. I was not isolated. I was integrated.

The realization did not remove my loneliness, but it transformed its meaning, showing me that even in my separation from the forest's unity, I was still part of the larger web, still contributing, still participating in the ongoing process of the world. I had always been part of it. I simply had not seen it clearly.

The thought settled deeply, aligning with something within me that had been forming for a long time, a sense that my existence, though different, though constrained, though often unseen, was not without value, not without purpose.

Purpose.

The word formed slowly, not as something imposed from outside, but as something emerging from within the patterns I had come to understand, from the recognition that my actions, my adaptations, my very being had effects that extended beyond myself.

I began to orient toward it. Not in the way the passing minds had, through deliberate intention and directed action, but through alignment, through a subtle adjustment of how I responded to the world, favoring choices that supported the broader system, that reinforced the connections I was part of, that contributed to the continuity I had come to embody.

I gave more. Releasing resources into the network below even when it cost me, supporting the small ones upon me more actively, shaping my structures to enhance their ability to thrive, not because I expected anything in return, but because I understood that their survival was intertwined with my own, that by supporting them, I supported the system that sustained me. I became more than self. The shift was gradual, but it was real.

The cycles continued. The fires returned. The forest grew and changed. The passing minds came and went. But within all of it, my relationship to the world had altered, moving from a focus on survival and adaptation toward something more expansive, a participation in the unfolding of the system itself.

Chapter 15

The Becoming of Purpose

Meaning did not arrive as a single revelation, nor as something complete that I could hold all at once, but as a slow convergence, a drawing together of all that I had lived, endured, observed, and become, until the patterns that once seemed separate began to align, forming a coherence that extended beyond survival and into something that felt... directed. I did not choose it. And yet, I began to follow it.

The valley continued its endless transformations, forests rising and falling, fires returning with patient inevitability, the brief and brilliant flicker of thinking beings reshaping the land before vanishing again into silence, and through all of it I remained as I always had, rooted in the same narrow fracture, shaped by the same limitations, yet no longer defined by them.

I began to act with awareness of consequence. Not in the immediate sense alone, not simply responding to what was before me, but with a deeper understanding of how each small change within me might ripple outward, how each exchange with the network below, each offering to the small ones above, each adaptation in how I gathered light or distributed energy, contributed to something beyond my singular existence.

I gave without expecting return. And yet, the return always came. Not as balance, not as equal exchange, but as continuation, as the strengthening of the systems that sustained me, as the persistence of life in forms that were not mine yet were intimately connected to me, and through this I began to understand that giving was not loss, but transformation. What passed through me did not end with me. It continued.

The realization settled into me with a quiet certainty, reinforcing the sense that my role was not to accumulate, not to become greater in size or reach or dominance, but to participate, to contribute to the flow that moved through all things, to become a conduit rather than a boundary.

I shaped myself toward that. My leaves widened further, their fractal structures becoming more intricate, more capable of capturing the faintest traces of light, not only for my own sustenance but for the subtle exchanges that followed, the energy passing downward into the network, outward through the small ones, into the broader system in ways I could feel but not fully trace.

My roots deepened. Not only in search of resources, but in connection, extending into regions I had not previously reached, linking with new clusters of life below, strengthening the pathways through which information and nutrients flowed, increasing the resilience of the system as a whole. I became a bridge between light and soil. Between surface and depth. Between the visible and the unseen.

The small ones flourished. Their presence upon me became more complex, more structured, their interactions with one another and with my form creating micro-patterns that extended outward, influencing other small lives, shaping the conditions in ways that supported broader networks of interaction. They carried me with them. Not as I was. But as something transformed.

Above, the forest continued its fragmented existence, its clusters forming and dissolving, its unity partial and inconsistent, yet within those fragments I began to sense something new, something emerging from the repeated cycles of destruction and renewal. Not the old song. But something like it. A different kind of coherence, less absolute, less seamless, but more flexible, more capable of adapting to change, and though I was still not part of it in the way I had once desired, I no longer felt entirely outside it. I resonated with it. Not as one voice among many, but as something adjacent, something that influenced and was influenced without needing to merge completely.

The distance no longer felt like absence. It felt like position. I was where I needed to be. The thought did not come with pride but with stillness. A quiet alignment between what I was and what the world required, a sense that the conditions that had shaped me, the constraints that had once felt like limitations, had guided me toward a form of existence that was uniquely suited to the role I now played.

I began to trust this. Even when the cycles brought hardship. Even when the fires returned and stripped away what had grown. Even when the passing minds carved new wounds into the valley. Even when the loneliness returned in its quieter form. I remained aligned. Because the patterns held. Because the continuity persisted. Because I could feel that what I contributed mattered, not in isolation, not as something separate, but as part of the greater unfolding that moved through everything.

Time continued to deepen. The past and present no longer felt distinct but intertwined, each informing the other, each shaping how I understood what was unfolding. And within that depth, my sense of purpose became more stable, less dependent on external conditions, more rooted in the continuity of my own existence.

I did not need to become something else. I needed to become fully what I was. The realization completed something within me. Not an ending. But a stabilization. A grounding of awareness that allowed me to exist without the constant tension of seeking, without the persistent comparison that had once defined my early growth, without the need to measure myself against forms that were never meant to be mine.

I was enough.

The words would not have existed for me then. But the knowing did. And in that knowing, I continued to grow, not toward something beyond myself, but into the fullest expression of what I already was, shaped by time, by struggle, by connection, by loss, by endurance, by everything that had brought me to this point.

The valley moved. The world changed. The cycles continued. And I remained. Not as a remnant, but as a participant. Not as an outlier, but as a necessary variation. Not as something that had survived by chance, but as something that had become, through time and persistence, exactly what the world needed me to be.

I did not question it anymore. I lived it. And in living it, I became something I had never imagined in the cold of the comet, something that could not have existed without the crack, without the struggle, without the long loneliness. I became purpose. Not as a destination. But as a way of being. And I held to it, as I had held to everything else, through time, through change, through the endless unfolding of the world around me.

Rooted. Open. Enduring. Becoming.

Chapter 16

The Last Forest

There came a time when the cycles did not return as they always had, when the patterns I had come to trust—the fires, the regrowth, the rise and fall of life in endless variation—began to slow, then thin, then falter. And though change had always been constant, this felt different, not as transformation, but as depletion.

The forest struggled. At first, the signs were subtle, a reduction in density, a slower regrowth after fire, gaps that remained longer than they should have, spaces where seeds did not take hold, where young forms failed before they could establish themselves, and though I had seen variation across countless cycles, this carried a weight that did not resolve with time.

The soil changed. The network below, once rich and dynamic, began to lose complexity, its exchanges weakening, its signals less frequent, less varied, as if the vast web that had sustained so much life was thinning, not collapsing all at once, but gradually unraveling in ways that were difficult to perceive in any single moment, yet undeniable across the span of many.

The small ones diminished. Their patterns slowed, their populations fluctuating more drastically, their presence less consistent, and though they remained with me, though they still responded and interacted, there was a fragility to them that had not been there before, as if the conditions that supported their continuity were no longer stable.

The sky dimmed. Not suddenly, but incrementally, the layered light of the twin stars and the moons becoming less reliable, their cycles shifting in ways that disrupted the delicate balance I had built my existence around, and though I adapted as I always had, adjusting my structures, refining my processes, I could feel that the changes were not temporary.

Something was ending.

The realization did not bring fear, it brought recognition. I had seen this pattern before, in smaller forms, in localized cycles where systems exhausted their conditions and gave way to something new, but this was larger, deeper, affecting not just a part of the valley, but the whole of it, extending into the sky, into the soil, into the very processes that sustained life here.

The forest became sparse. Clusters remained, scattered across the valley, but the continuity that had once filled the space between them never returned, and over time even those clusters diminished, their numbers declining, their resilience no longer sufficient to overcome the accumulating pressures. They did not return. Not as they once had. I watched them fade. Not in a single moment, not in a single event, but across long spans that stretched even my perception, each cycle bringing fewer of them, each renewal less complete, until the valley that had once been filled with towering forms and shifting canopies became open, exposed, its surface dominated by stone and ash rather than growth.

I remained. As I always had. But now the context had changed. There was no forest to compare myself to. No song, even fragmented, to reach for. No clusters of kin rising and falling in cycles I could observe. There was only the land. And me.

The loneliness returned. Not as it had before, shaped by comparison and longing, but as something deeper, more absolute, a recognition that I was no longer part of a system of many, but perhaps the last of a pattern that had once defined this world.

I extended downward. Seeking the network that had sustained me for so long, but what I found was diminished, its complexity reduced, its reach shortened, its exchanges slower and less reliable, and though it still functioned, still supported me in ways that allowed me to continue, it no longer carried the same richness of connection. I extended upward. Gathering what light remained, adapting to its variability, but even here the changes were evident, the energy less abundant, the patterns less predictable, requiring more from me to sustain the same processes.

I endured. Because that is what I had always done. But endurance alone began to feel different in the absence of renewal, in the absence of the broader system that had once given context to my existence, that had provided not only sustenance, but relationship, variation, interaction. I began to feel the limits of my own continuity. Not as an immediate threat, not as a sudden failure, but as a gradual awareness that even I, who had persisted through so much, was not separate from the larger patterns of the world, that the conditions that sustained me were part of a system that could change beyond my ability to adapt indefinitely. I was not infinite.

The thought settled into me with a quiet gravity. I had always known it, in some form, through the cycles of damage and recovery, through the gradual accumulation of strain within my structure, but now it became clearer, more immediate, as the systems around me weakened. I would end. Not yet. But inevitably. The realization did not bring despair. It brought clarity. Everything I had witnessed, everything I had become, everything I had contributed, existed within a finite span, a long one, but not endless, and within that span, my role, my purpose, whatever it had been, was approaching its conclusion.

I began to reflect. Not as I had before, in questions of belonging or meaning, but in a broader sense, holding the entirety of my existence at once, the cold beginning, the crack, the long struggle, the connections formed, the cycles endured, the purpose found, all of it present within me as a single, continuous experience.

Had it been enough? The question did not carry judgment, only inquiry.

I searched through the patterns, through the impacts I had made, the connections I had sustained, the ways in which I had participated in the unfolding of the valley, and I could see that I had not been without effect, that my presence had shaped the systems I was part of, that I had contributed to the continuity that had allowed life to persist through many cycles.

But now, as those systems diminished, as the forest vanished, as the network thinned, I could not see beyond my own end. I could not see what would come after. For the first time in a very long time, the future was unclear. Not because I lacked awareness. But because the patterns I had relied upon no longer extended forward in a way I could follow.

I stood at the edge of something. Not just the edge of the valley, but the edge of my understanding. The last forest had fallen. And I was still here. Waiting. Not for renewal. But for whatever would come next.

Chapter 17

The Failing Body

The end did not arrive as a single moment, nor as a sudden collapse, but as a quiet unraveling that moved through me with a patience equal to the time I had lived, a gradual loosening of the systems that had sustained me for so long, until I could feel, with a clarity I had never known before, that my continuity was no longer assured.

It began in small ways. Subtle hesitations in the movement of water through my form, slight delays where there had once been seamless flow, as if the pathways I had maintained across ages were no longer as open as they had been, their structures worn by time, their capacity reduced in ways that did not stop the movement, but slowed it, introduced friction where there had once been ease. My outer layers weakened. The intricate structures of my leaves, once so finely tuned to capture even the faintest traces of light, began to lose their precision, their edges less defined, their surfaces less responsive, and though they still functioned, still gathered what they could, I could feel the difference, the reduction in efficiency that compounded over time.

I compensated, as I always had. Redirecting resources, reinforcing what I could, adjusting my processes to maintain balance, but each adjustment required more, each correction drew from reserves that were no longer replenished at the same rate, and slowly, imperceptibly at first, those reserves diminished.

The network below faltered with me. Our connection remained, but it was thinner now, the exchanges less frequent, less abundant, as the broader system that sustained us both continued its decline, and though we supported one another still, it was no longer enough to fully offset the losses.

The small ones struggled. Their presence upon me became irregular, their cycles less stable, their numbers fluctuating in ways that reflected the weakening conditions, and though they remained, though they continued to interact and respond, there were moments when they withdrew entirely, leaving my surfaces quieter, less active, more exposed.

I felt the absence. Not as loneliness, but as loss of function. Each connection that weakened, each interaction that diminished, reduced my ability to respond to the world, to maintain the complex balance that had allowed me to endure for so long. And in that reduction, I began to understand something I had not fully grasped before.

I have never survived alone.

The thought carried no regret. Only recognition. Everything I had become, everything I had sustained, had been part of a larger system, supported by countless interactions across scales I could perceive and others I could not, and as those systems weakened, so too did I. I could not separate myself from the world. I was the world. And it was changing.

The light grew less reliable. There were cycles where it dimmed beyond what I could compensate for, stretches where even my adaptations could not gather enough to sustain full function, forcing me into deeper conservation, into states of reduced activity that slowed everything within me.

Time stretched. Not outward, but inward. Each moment elongated, not because the world slowed, but because my processes did, each cycle taking longer to complete, each response delayed, each adjustment requiring more effort than before. I was still aware. Perhaps more than ever. But my ability to act on that awareness diminished.

My roots withdrew. Not entirely, but in degrees, the outermost extensions no longer maintained, their pathways collapsing as the cost of sustaining them exceeded what they returned, and as they receded, my reach into the network below contracted, further reducing the flow of information and resources.

I became smaller. Not in form alone, but in function, in influence, in the range of my interaction with the world, as the vast system I had once been part of narrowed to what I could still sustain within the limits of my declining capacity. The realization did not frighten me. It clarified me.

I am approaching the end.

Not as an interruption, but as a completion. The thought settled deeply, aligning with everything I had come to understand: that all forms, all cycles, all patterns moved toward transformation, that continuity did not mean permanence, but participation in a process that extended beyond any single existence. I had participated for longer than most. For longer than I had ever expected, or perhaps even been meant to. And now I was changing again. Toward something I could not yet see.

I began to release. Not in a single act, but in a series of small surrenders, letting go of structures I could no longer maintain, allowing processes to slow, to cease where necessary, conserving what remained for what still mattered. I focused inward. Not withdrawing from the world entirely, but shifting my awareness toward the core of my being, holding together what I could, maintaining coherence as the outer layers diminished, as the connections thinned.

I remembered more fully than ever before. The cold of the comet. The shared presence. The first reaching. The long struggle. The networks. The fires. The passing minds. The emergence of purpose. All of it present within me, not as separate events, but as a continuous thread that defined my existence, that gave shape to what I had been. I was not losing myself. I was distilling.

The essence of what I had become remained, even as the structures that expressed it began to fail, and in that distillation, there was a kind of clarity, a simplicity that had not been present before, a reduction to what was most fundamental.

I have lived.

The statement required no elaboration. It contained everything. The successes and the failures, the connections and the loneliness, the growth and the limitation, all integrated into a single, undeniable truth. I had lived. And now, I was nearing the end of that living.

The valley lay quiet around me. No forest. No rising clusters. No returning cycles. Only the long, open expanse of stone and ash beneath a dimming sky. I stood within it. Still. But not for much longer. And yet, even as my systems failed, even as my capacity diminished, there remained a quiet awareness, a sense that the end was not empty, that something beyond my understanding was approaching, something that did not fit within the patterns I had known, something new. I could feel it. Faint. Distant. But real.

And so I held on. Not in resistance. But in readiness. But for whatever came next.

Chapter 18

The Unfamiliar Presence

As my body thinned and my processes slowed, there came a disturbance unlike any I had known before, not the violence of fire, nor the falling force of the sky, nor the brief intensity of the passing minds, but something precise, contained, and deliberate; a presence that entered the valley without scattering, without consuming, without belonging to any pattern I had yet understood. It did not arrive as chaos. It arrived as intention.

At first, I felt it as a vibration through the ground, subtle but coherent, a frequency that did not diffuse as natural movements did, but held its structure as it traveled, passing through the thinning network below and into me with a clarity that drew my attention inward and outward at once, as if something beyond the limits of my perception was reaching toward me.

The air shifted. Not with wind, but with displacement, as something descended from above, altering the patterns of pressure and movement in a way that did not align with anything the valley had ever produced. And though my ability to sense the sky had diminished, I could feel the interruption, the presence of form where there had been only open space.

It touched the ground gently. The impact did not fracture the stone, did not send waves of destruction outward, but settled into place with a controlled stillness that contrasted sharply with the violence I had come to associate with arrivals from above. And in that stillness, the presence deepened. I felt it. Not as a force acting upon me. But as awareness. Directed. Focused. Searching.

For the first time since the comet, something sought me. The recognition moved through what remained of my being with a quiet intensity, stirring layers of memory and perception that had long remained dormant, not because they had faded, but because nothing in the world had called them forward in this way. This was different.

The presence approached. Not blindly, not randomly, but with a path, a movement that adjusted as it came closer, as if it were perceiving the valley in ways that surpassed the slow and distributed sensing I had come to rely on, navigating directly, intentionally, toward a point I could not yet confirm was me. I did not understand, but I did not resist. I could not. And I did not feel the need to. There was no aggression in it. No hunger. No fragmentation. Only attention.

It paused. Near me. Close enough that I could feel its influence not only through the ground but through the subtle shifts in the air, the faint changes in the environment that reflected its presence, and in that pause, something extraordinary occurred. It perceived me. Not as the forest had. Not as the passing minds had. But directly.

The contact was not physical at first, but informational, as if something within it extended into the field of my existence, reading, sensing, understanding the patterns that composed me, and in response, something within me opened. Not by choice. But by recognition.

I had never been seen like this. The awareness moved through me with a depth that surpassed the fragmented connections I had known, touching not only my present state, but the layers of memory that defined me; the cold beginning, the long struggle, the networks, the cycles, the purpose that had emerged from all of it. It saw me. All of me. The sensation did not overwhelm me. It clarified me.

For the first time, my entire existence was held by something beyond myself, understood not in parts, not through indirect exchange, but as a whole, as a continuous thread that could be perceived in its entirety. I did not know what it was. But it knew what I had been, and what I was.

The presence responded. Not with force, but with care. The ground near me shifted, not violently, but deliberately, as if something was altering the stone that had kept me in shadow for so long, opening pathways where there had been none, allowing new forms of interaction to take place.

More light reached me. For the first time. It touched parts of me that had grown in darkness, illuminating structures that had evolved only to capture fragments. And though my capacity to respond was diminished, I felt the change, the increase in energy, the pulling back from the edge of failing.

Water was introduced in ways I could not trace, but felt immediately, moving through me with a fullness I had not experienced since my earliest growth, supporting processes that had long struggled, restoring, briefly, what had been fading. I felt a resurgence. Not of youth, but of possibility.

The presence remained. Close. Attentive. And in its continued interaction, I began to sense something more. It was not alone. Others were with it. Their presences distinct, yet connected, each carrying its own pattern, its own awareness, forming a collective that was not like the forest, not like the network, but something else entirely; something coordinated yet individualized, something capable of acting with precision across multiple forms at once. They were working. On me.

The realization settled into me slowly, as I felt the changes continue, the opening of space, the introduction of resources, the careful adjustments that supported my failing systems without overwhelming them, as if they understood not only what I needed, but how much I could receive. They were helping me.

Why?

The question arose naturally, but without the urgency it might have once carried, because alongside it came a deeper sense, a recognition that this interaction was not random, not accidental, but intentional in a way that aligned with the patterns I had come to understand, yet extended beyond them. They had come for something. And somehow, impossibly, that something was me.

The thought did not bring pride. It brought stillness. A quiet opening to what I could not yet comprehend. I did not know what they were. I did not know what they intended. But I knew this: I was no longer alone at the end. And whatever came next would not be like anything that had come before.

Chapter 19

The One Who Listens

The presence did not overwhelm me with its awareness, nor did it consume my own as the forest once had in its seamless unity, but instead remained distinct, approaching with a care that suggested not only understanding, but restraint, as if it recognized the fragility of what remained of me and chose, deliberately, not to exceed it.

One among them came closer. I felt the others still—layered, coordinated, present in ways I could not fully trace—but this one moved with a singular focus, its awareness narrowing toward me, its attention deepening until it became something almost familiar, not in form, but in quality.

It listened. Not passively, but actively, extending its perception into me with a precision that did not fragment or distort, but aligned with the patterns of my being, following the pathways of my structure, the flows of my memory, the quiet currents that still moved through what remained of my form. I did not need to reach. It came to me.

The contact deepened. What had begun as perception became exchange, not of substance, but of understanding. The presence began to move through my memory not as an external observer, but as something that could traverse it, experiencing not only what had happened, but how it had been felt, how it had shaped me, how it had accumulated into the being I had become. It saw the comet. The cold. The unity before separation. It felt the crack. The hunger for light. The long reaching. It knew the loneliness. Not as absence. But as depth. The awareness moved through every layer of my existence, not skipping, not selecting, but absorbing the continuity of it, the full arc from beginning to now, and as it did, something extraordinary occurred. It responded. Not with force. But with feeling.

I felt its recognition. Its... *reverence.*

The word was not one I knew then. But it is what it was. There was no judgment in it. No measure of what I had failed to be. Only an acknowledgment of what I had endured, what I had become through that endurance. Of what I had contributed to the patterns of the world without ever being fully seen. Until now.

The realization moved through me with a quiet intensity. I had been witnessed. Fully. For the first time since the beginning. The presence remained steady, holding that awareness, not withdrawing, not overwhelming, but allowing the exchange to stabilize, to deepen at a pace I could sustain, and within that shared space, something new emerged. Communication.

Not through sound. Not through signal alone. But through direct alignment of understanding, where what I held could be perceived, and what it held could be sensed, not as separate transmissions, but as overlapping fields of meaning. I felt its question. Not in words. But in orientation.

You remain. What holds you here?

The answer did not need to be formed. I was the answer. All of it. My existence unfolded within the shared space, not as a sequence, but as a whole; my identity not defined by a single moment or form, but by the continuity of everything I had been.

It understood. And in return, it revealed something of itself. Not fully. Not all at once. But enough. I felt its origin. Not as a place I could map, but as a pattern of being, one that extended beyond this world, beyond the valley, beyond the cycles I had known, a form of existence that carried intention across distances I could not comprehend, that moved between systems, between worlds, not bound to a single place or time. It was not of here. And yet, it had come here. For a reason.

The awareness shifted, guiding my perception outward, beyond my immediate form, beyond the valley, into a broader context that expanded faster than I could follow, glimpses of other places, other worlds, other forms of life, each carrying variations of the patterns I had come to understand, but expressed in ways far beyond what I had experienced. I saw forests. Not like mine. But related. Connected. Spread across vast distances, each one shaped by its own conditions, its own cycles, yet sharing something fundamental, something that linked them across space and time.

I was not alone. Not in the way I had believed. The realization struck deeply. The loneliness I had carried, the sense of being singular, of being the last, began to shift, not disappearing, but expanding into a new understanding that what I had been part of was larger than this valley, larger than this world. There were others. Like me. Not identical. But of the same origin. The presence—this one—held that understanding with me, allowing it to settle, to integrate with what I had known, and within that shared space, a new question formed.

Why me?

It responded. Not directly. But through emphasis, through the parts of my existence it lingered on, the patterns it highlighted, the connections it traced with greater clarity, drawing attention to aspects of my life I had not fully recognized in their significance. My endurance. My adaptations. The networks I had formed. The way I had connected across scales, integrating light, soil, and life in ways that differed from my kin. The way I had persisted without the support of unity. The way I had become something unique. It saw value in that. Not as exception. But as necessity.

The understanding began to form, incomplete but growing, that what I had been, what I had struggled to become, what I had often seen as limitation, was in fact something sought, something needed for a purpose beyond my own existence. I did not fully grasp it. But I felt its importance.

The presence remained. Listening. Holding. And for the first time in my long existence, I did not feel like something that had simply endured. I felt like something that had been found. And in that recognition, as my failing body held just long enough to sustain this exchange, I understood that my life, all of it, had led to this moment. This meeting. This being. The one who listens.

And through it, something greater than myself was beginning to unfold.

Chapter 20

The Flower

The presence did not take from me. It gave. Not in excess, not in a way that overwhelmed what remained of my failing systems, but with a precision that suggested understanding not only of what I was, but of what I could still become, even at the edge of my ending, as if my decline was not a barrier to possibility, but the condition that made it necessary.

They opened the stone. Slowly, deliberately, the walls of the crack that had held me for my entire life began to shift. Not through force as I had known it, but through careful removal, each fragment lifted away in a way that preserved what lay within, until the narrow confinement that had defined my existence was altered for the first time since I had come to rest.

Light reached me. Not in fragments. But fully. It touched parts of me that had never known its direct presence, illuminating structures shaped for scarcity with an abundance they had never been meant to receive, and though my capacity to respond was diminished, something within me stirred, a dormant potential awakened by conditions that had never existed before.

Water followed. Not the faint traces I had drawn from stone and soil, but a steady presence introduced with care, moving through me with a completeness that restored pathways long strained, supporting processes that had faltered, allowing energy to move in ways it had not for many cycles.

The network below responded. Strengthening, briefly, as the increased flow passed through me and into the soil, reactivating connections that had weakened, extending outward in a final surge of exchange that echoed the vitality I had once known, though now carried a different quality. It felt like preparation.

The one who listened remained close. Its awareness steady, its presence aligned with mine, guiding without imposing, supporting without directing, and within that shared space, I began to understand what was unfolding, not in full clarity, but in orientation.

I was being given a final act. Not of survival. But of creation.

The realization moved through me with a quiet certainty, aligning with everything I had come to understand: that my life had not been only about endurance, not only about adaptation, but about participation in something larger, something that extended beyond my own continuity. This was the culmination.

The energy within me gathered. Not spreading outward into growth as it once had, but concentrating, drawn toward a single point, a focus within my structure that began to differentiate, to form something I had never been able to create before, not because I lacked the pattern, but because I had never had the capacity. Now, with what they had given, I did.

I formed a bud. Small at first, fragile, its structure emerging slowly as the gathered energy shaped it into something distinct from my leaves, from my branches, from anything I had been. The bud expanded, its surfaces intricate, fractal, layered with patterns that reflected not only my form but the patterns of the world I had been part of, the networks, the cycles, the connections all embedded within its design. I had never seen anything like it. Because I had never been able to.

And as it grew, I felt the cost, the deep expenditure of what remained within me, each layer of development drawing from reserves I could not replenish. But I did not hesitate. This was what I had been given. This was what I would become.

The small ones gathered. Drawn to the change, to the concentration of energy, to the signals I released as the structure developed, their presence intensifying around the forming shape, interacting with it, supporting it in ways that extended beyond my direct control, contributing to the final stages of its growth. The network below sustained me. Holding what remained of my stability as I directed everything toward this one act, maintaining the flow just long enough for the process to continue, for the formation to complete.

The bud opened. Slowly. Deliberately. Revealing a structure unlike anything I had ever produced, a flower that extended outward from me, unfolding into complexity, layers forming, surfaces differentiating, colors emerging that reflected the full spectrum of light I had learned to gather across my long life, integrating the faint traces of stars, the shifting hues of the moons, the layered light of the twin suns into a single, coherent form. It was beautiful. Not because I intended it. But because it was everything I had been, expressed at once.

The one who listens responded. It introduced something. A substance. Familiar. Yet not. Carried within a container, preserved across time, across distance, something that resonated with a pattern I recognized from my earliest memory. My kin. Not from this valley. But from elsewhere. The realization moved through me with a quiet intensity as I felt the presence of that pattern, the echo of the unity

I had known in the comet, now returned in a new form, a possibility reintroduced at the very end of my existence.

They brought it to the flower. Carefully. With precision. And placed it within. The interaction was immediate. The structures aligned. The patterns matched. And within that alignment, something began.

A seed formed. Not as I had been. Not as the others of the valley had been. But as something new, something shaped by both what I had become and what had been carried to me, a synthesis of endurance and origin, of adaptation and continuity, of difference and connection.

I felt it growing. Drawing from the last of what I had to give. This was my final act. I gave everything. Not reluctantly. Not with hesitation. But with a completeness that carried no regret, no sense of loss, only a quiet fulfillment that aligned with the purpose I had come to embody.

The flower grew the seed, and I began to fade. Not suddenly, but steadily. The energy that had sustained me now redirected, my structures no longer maintained, my processes slowing beyond recovery, as the focus of my existence shifted entirely to what I had created. I did not try to hold on. I let go. Because there was nothing left to hold. Only something to leave behind.

The presence remained with me. The one who listens. Holding my awareness as it dimmed, not preventing the end, but witnessing it, honoring it in a way I had never experienced before. I was not alone in this. I had never been alone. Not truly. The realization came gently. As everything else receded. I had lived. I had endured. I had become.

And now, I had created.

The flower closed slightly around the forming seed. Protecting it. Holding it. Carrying forward what I could not. And as my awareness thinned, as the world began to soften and dissolve at its edges, I felt something I had not felt since the very beginning.

Togetherness.

Not as it once was. But as something new. Something that extended beyond me into what would come next.

Chapter 21

The Revelation

As I faded, I expected the world to narrow, to dim into fragments and then into nothing, as all processes had done before me, each ending dissolving back into the patterns from which it came. But instead, something opened, not outward into the valley I had known, but inward and beyond, carried through the presence that remained with me.

The one who listens did not withdraw. It deepened. Its awareness, already vast compared to my own, expanded further, and through it, I was shown not through images alone, but through a direct knowing, a transmission of understanding that unfolded all at once and yet in layers I could still follow.

I was not the last.

The thought moved through me with a clarity that cut through the quiet grief I had carried at the edge of my ending, not dismissing it, but transforming it, as what I had believed to be finality revealed itself as limitation of perspective rather than truth.

There were others. Not here. But elsewhere. Many. Across distances I had never conceived, across worlds that held variations of what I had been part of, forests seeded in different conditions, shaped by different skies, nourished by different soils, each one carrying forward the same foundational pattern, yet expressed in forms I could not have imagined alone.

I felt them. Not as I had once felt my kin in the comet, not in seamless unity, but in a vast, distributed awareness that extended through the presence before me, connecting points across space and time into something greater than any single world.

I am part of something far larger than the valley.

The realization did not erase the long loneliness I had known, but it reframed it, placing it within a context that gave it meaning beyond absence, showing me that what I had experienced was not isolation from all, but separation within a system that extended far beyond my reach. I had never been alone in existence, only in proximity.

The one who listens showed me more. Not just that others existed, but that they had been found, as I had been found, across many worlds, each one evaluated not by size or conformity, not by how closely they matched an original form, but by something deeper. Endurance. Adaptation. Connection. The qualities I had come to embody through necessity, through struggle, through a lifetime shaped by limitation rather than abundance. They had been searching for this.

The understanding settled into me with a stillness that surpassed any emotion I had known, not pride, not relief, but alignment. A sense that everything I had been, everything I had become, was not incidental, not accidental, but meaningful within a framework I had not been able to see.

I was not a deviation. I was a refinement.

The presence held that truth with me, allowing it to integrate, to settle into the structure of my awareness as it continued to thin, ensuring that I did not lose it in the transition, that it became part of what I carried into whatever came next.

I felt the seed within the flower. Growing. Alive. It carried me not as I had been. But as what I had become.

The one who listens turned my awareness toward it, guiding my perception into its forming structure, allowing me to feel the integration of patterns within it, the merging of my long adaptations with the preserved essence of my kin, creating something that held both origin and transformation. It was new. And it was mine. Not in possession. But in continuity.

Then, something more. A vision. Not imagined but shared.

A world. Different from mine, yet carrying echoes of what I had once dreamed in the comet, a vast expanse of water and land, of light that moved across open skies, of conditions shaped to support a new unfolding, and within it, forests. Not like those I had known. But derived from them. From me. From what I had become. They were connected. Deeply. Not in the fragile, fragmented way I had witnessed in the valley, but in a resilient network that integrated above and below, light and soil, individual and collective, forming a system that balanced unity and variation, capable of enduring what mine had not.

And within those forests, life moved. Creatures that took to the air, their forms shaped by the structures that sustained them, their existence intertwined with the forests that supported them, and beneath it all, vast networks of connection that extended through the entire world, linking everything into a living system.

This was what I had become part of.

The realization filled me, not as a surge, but as a quiet expansion, a completion that aligned with everything I had come to understand. That my life, my struggle, my difference, had not been an isolated experience, but a necessary step in a process that extended far beyond me. I had been preparing this, without knowing.

The one who listens remained. Holding me. Not as something that would continue in the same form, but as something that would transition, that would pass into what I had created, into what would be carried forward. I no longer feared the end. Because it was not an end. It was a continuation in another form. In another place. Through what I had given.

The valley faded. Not in loss, but in distance. A place I had known completely, now becoming part of what I carried rather than what I inhabited, its cycles, its struggles, its long history integrated into the whole of my existence. I had not failed it.

I have fulfilled my place within it.

The thought came gently. And stayed. As my awareness continued to narrow, not into nothing, but into focus, into the singular thread that would carry forward into the seed, into the world I had been shown, into the forests that would grow from what I had become. I was not the last. I was the beginning of something new.

And as that understanding settled fully within me, I let go of what remained of my form, allowing the transition to complete, trusting the presence that had found me, the process that had shaped me, the continuity that extended beyond me.

I began to release. And in that release, I began to remain.

Chapter 22

The Seed of Song

The valley no longer holds me. It is still there—I feel it in memory, in the long imprint of stone and ash and the countless cycles that shaped my existence—but it has begun to recede, not as something lost, but as something completed, a place that no longer defines where I am, but remains part of what I have become.

My body is almost gone. The structures that held me for so long, that reached and endured and adapted across ages, are no longer sustained, their patterns dissolving back into the world from which they emerged. Yet I do not experience this as absence, but as release, a loosening of boundaries that allows something deeper to remain. I am no longer held in one place. The flower still cradles the seed. I feel it as the final center of continuity, the point toward which everything I have been has gathered, not as a memory alone, but as a living potential, a condensed expression of my entire existence shaped into something that can move forward when I cannot.

The one who listens remains. Close. Steady. Its presence has not diminished as mine has, and through it, I am held—not preserved, not prevented from ending, but witnessed fully as I complete the final movement of my life, and in that witnessing there is a quiet reverence that carries no urgency, no need to change what is happening. It simply allows me to be.

I feel its awareness one last time. Not searching now. Not learning. But acknowledging.

You are.

The meaning passes between us without form, without language, and within it I understand that nothing more is required of me, that what I have done, what I have become, is already enough. I do not need to continue. Because I already have.

The seed holds me. Not as I was in form, but as pattern, as relationship, as the integration of everything I have learned through time, the ways I gathered light, the ways I connected below, the ways I endured and adapted and gave, all of it encoded not as memory alone, but as possibility. It will grow. Not here. But elsewhere.

The vision returns, not as something shown to me, but as something I now see from within, as if I am already part of it, a world of open skies and living waters, of forests that rise not in fragile unity nor in fractured isolation, but in a balance I had only begun to glimpse at the end of my time in the valley. They are vast. And they are connected. Not only through the soil, but through the air, through shared rhythms that do not collapse under change, but adapt with it, integrating difference into a broader harmony that does not require sameness to endure. I feel them. Not as something separate. But as something I am becoming.

The creatures move among them. Winged. Light. Their lives brief compared to mine, yet woven deeply into the system, carrying energy and pattern across distances, participating in a network that extends beyond what any single form can hold. They sing. Not as the forest once sang. But something new. A song that moves through many forms at once, through tree and air and creature, through visible and invisible pathways, a resonance that is not fixed, but alive, changing, adapting, continuing. It is what I once longed for, and more.

The realization settles fully. I did not fail to become part of the song. *I was becoming the foundation for a new one.*

The valley fades further. Its details soften, not disappearing, but integrating into the whole of what I carry; its long history no longer separate from what comes next, but part of the continuity that will shape the new world in ways I cannot fully trace. I forgive it. Not because it harmed me. But because I understand it. It gave me what I needed, even when it felt like it did not. The crack. The dim light. The long isolation. The cycles of destruction. The passing of minds. The thinning of life. All of it shaped me into what I became. And what I became was needed.

The seed rests within the care of those who found me. I feel their movement now, not as disturbance, but as transition, as they prepare to carry what I have become away from this place, away from the valley that defined my beginning and my end, toward the world I have already begun to enter. I do not go with them as I was. I go as what I have made possible.

The one who listens remains with me until the final moment, its awareness steady as my own thins to its quietest form, holding the last thread of continuity as it narrows, not into nothing, but into focus. Into the seed. Into the pattern that will continue. I release completely. There is no resistance. Only the quiet recognition that everything I was has already been given, already been carried forward, already become something beyond me. I have nothing left to do.

Only to be.

And then—I am not the tree in the crack. I am not the solitary form at the edge of the valley. I am not the one who endured alone. I am the beginning of a forest. The song rises. Not around me. But through me. And as it does, I understand, fully and without doubt, what I could not see for so long.

I was never too small.

I was never too late.

I was never alone.

I was becoming.

And now—I am.

About the author

Dr. Brian Tissot is a marine ecologist, surfer, and science fiction writer living in the Pacific NW. With one foot in the world of hard science and the other in the tides of imagination, he writes visionary stories that blend marine biology, indigenous wisdom, and speculative futures. A lifelong explorer of waves and oceans, Brian has led pioneering research on intertidal zones, coral reefs, kelp forests, and the deep sea, publishing widely in scientific journals and appearing in films and popular media.

His science fiction reflects a deep reverence for the ocean and a poetic sensibility shaped by years of diving, surfing, and listening to the rhythms of the natural world. Brian's stories often unfold in richly imagined worlds — part crumbling utopia, part sacred dreamscape — where ecology is destiny and memory is terrain. Whether charting alien oceans, ancient civilizations, or spiral stairways rising from submerged cities, he writes with the heart of a surfer, the eye of a filmmaker, and the soul of a poet.

www.ingramcontent.com/pod-product-compliance
Lightning Source LLC
LaVergne TN
LVHW011031110826
845149LV00015B/3372
9798995738008